ONCE
UPON A
SUMMER

ONCE UPON A SUMMER

JANETTE OKE

JO

ONCE UPON A SUMMER
A Bethany House Publication/July 1981
The Janette Oke Collection/1997

Cover by Dan Thornberg, Bethany House staff artist.

Bethany House Publishers
A Ministry of Bethany Fellowship, Inc.
11300 Hampshire Avenue South
Minneapolis, Minnesota 55438

If you would be interested in purchasing additional copies of this book,
please write to this address for information:

The Janette Oke Collection
BDD Direct, Inc.
1540 Broadway
New York, NY 10036

ISBN: 0-553-80561-4

BDD Direct, Inc., 1540 Broadway, New York, New York 10036

Printed in the United States of America

1   3   5   7   9   10   8   6   4   2

Dedicated with love to
Fred and Amy (Ruggles) Steeves,
my dear parents,
who have given me
unmeasured love and support.

Table of Contents

Chapter 1

Josh

I could hardly wait to finish my chores that mornin'. I needed to sneak off to my favorite log along the crik bank and find myself some thinkin' time. Too many things had been happening too fast; I was worried that my whole world was about to change. I didn't want it changed. I liked things jest the way they were, but if I was to keep 'em that way, it was going to take some figurin' out.

I toted the pail of milk to the house and ran back to the barn to let Bossie back out to pasture to run with the range cows. She just mosied along, so I tried to hurry her along a bit, but she didn't pay much notice. Finally she went through the gate; I slapped her brown-and-white rump and hurried to lift the bars in place. Bossie jest stood there, seeming undecided as to where to go now that the choice was hers.

Me, I knew where I was headin'. I took off down the south trail, between the summer's green leafy things, like a rabbit with a hawk at its back.

The crik was still high, it being the middle of summer, but the spot that I called mine was a quiet place. Funny how one *feels* it quiet, even though there isn't a still moment down by the crik. One bird song followed another, and all sorts of bugs buzzed continually. Occasionally a frog would croak from the shallows or a fish would jump in the deeper waters. That kind of noise didn't bother me, though. I still found the spot restful, mostly 'cause there weren't any human voices biddin' ya to do this or git that.

I sorta regarded this spot as my own private fish hole; I hadn't even shared it with my best friend, Avery Garrett. Avery wasn't much for fishin' anyway, so he didn't miss the information. Today I never even thought to stop to grab my pole—I was that keen on gettin' off alone.

Even before I finally sat down on my log, I had rolled my overall legs up to near my knees and let my feet slip into the cool crik water. I pushed my feet down deep, stretchin' my toes through the thin layer of coarse sand so I could wiggle them around in the mud beneath. Too late I saw that my overalls hadn't been rolled up high enough and were soaking up crik water. I pulled at them, but being wet they didn't slide up too well. I'd get spoken to about that unless the sun got the dryin' job done before I got home. I sat there, wigglin' my toes and trying to decide jest what angle to come at my problems from.

Seemed to me that everything had gone along jest great until yesterday. Yesterday had started out okay, too. Grandpa needed to go to town, and he called to me right after I'd finished my chores.

"Boy." He most always called me Boy rather than Joshua, or even Josh, like other folks did. "Boy, ya be carin' fer a trip to town with me?"

I didn't even answer—jest grinned—'cause I knew that Grandpa already knew the answer anyway. I went to town every chance I got.

"Be ready in ten minutes," Grandpa said and went out for the team.

Wasn't much work to get ready. I washed my face and hands again, slicked down my hair and checked my overalls for dirt. They looked all right to me, so I scampered for the barn, hoping to get in on the hitchin' up of the horses.

The trip to town was quiet. Grandpa and I both enjoyed silence. Besides, there really wasn't that much that needed sayin'—and why talk jest to make a sound? Grandpa broke the quiet spell.

"Gettin' a little dry."

I looked at the ditches and could see brown spots where shortly before everything had been green and growin'. I nodded.

We went on into town and Grandpa stopped the team at the front of Kirk's General Store. I hopped down and hitched the team to the rail while Grandpa sort of gathered himself together for what needed to be done.

Soon we were inside the store and after exchangin' "howdys" and small-town talk with Mr. Kirk and some customers, Grandpa and I set about our business. Grandpa's was easy enough. He was to purchase the supplies needed back at the farm. I had a tougher job. Before I'd left, Uncle Charlie had, as usual, slipped me a nickel on the sly; now I had to decide how to spend it. I moved along the counter to get a better look at what Mr. Kirk had to offer. Mrs. Kirk was toward the back talkin' to someone over the telephone. Only a few folks in town had telephones; I never could get used to watching someone talkin' into a box. She finally quit and walked over to me.

"Mornin', Daniel. Nice day again, isn't it? Fear it's gonna be a bit hot afore it's over, though."

Without even waiting for a reply, she said to Grandpa, "Wanted to be sure that ya got this letter that came fer ya."

Mrs. Kirk ran our local post office from a back corner of the general store. She was a pleasant woman, and her concern for people was jest that—concern rather than idle curiosity.

Grandpa took the letter, his face lighting up as he did so. We didn't get much mail out our way.

"From my pa," he volunteered, giving Mrs. Kirk his rather lopsided grin. "Thank ya, ma'am." He stuffed the letter into his shirt pocket.

I forgot about the letter and went back to the business of spending my nickel. It seemed it was next-to-no-time when

Grandpa was gathering his purchases and askin' me if I was about ready to go. I still hadn't made up my mind.

I finally settled on a chocolate ice-cream cone, then went to help Grandpa with the packages. I wasn't much good to him, havin' one hand occupied, but I did the best I could.

He backed the team out and we headed for home, me makin' every lick count—that ice cream plum disappears in summer weather. When we were clear of the town, Grandpa handed the reins to me.

"I'm kinda anxious to see what my pa be sayin'," he explained as he pulled the letter from his shirt pocket. He read in silence and I stole a glance at him now and then. I wanted to find out how a letter written jest to you would make a body feel. This one didn't seem to be pleasin' my grandpa much. Finally he folded it slowly and tucked it into the envelope, then turned to me.

"Yer great-granny jest passed away, Boy."

Funny that at that moment he connected her with me instead of himself. He reached for the reins again in an absent-minded way. If he'd really been thinkin', he would have let me keep drivin'—he most often did on the way back from town.

I watched him out of the corner of my eye. I was sorry to hear about Great-granny, but I couldn't claim to sorrow. I had never met her and had heard very little about her. Suddenly it hit me that it was different for Grandpa. That faraway old lady who had jest died was his ma. I felt a lump come up in my throat then—a kind of feelin' fer Grandpa—but I didn't know how to tell him how I felt.

Grandpa was deep in thought. He didn't even seem to be aware of the reins that lay slack in his hands. I was sure that I could have reached over and taken them back and he never would have noticed. I didn't though. I jest sat there quiet-like and let the thoughts go through his mind. I could imagine right then that Grandpa was rememberin' Great-granny as he had seen her last. Many times he'd told me that when he was fifteen, he'd decided that he wanted to get away from the city. So he had packed up the few things that were rightly his, bid good-bye to his folks and struck out for the West. Great-granny had cried as she watched him go, but she hadn't tried to stop him. Grandpa had been west for many years, had a farm, a wife and a family, when he invited Uncle Charlie, his older and only brother, to join him. Uncle Charlie was a bachelor and Grandpa needed the extra hands fer the crops and hayin'. Uncle Charlie had been only too glad to leave his job as a hardware-store clerk and travel west to join Grandpa.

Every year or so the two of them would sit and talk about hopping a train and payin' a visit "back home," but they never did git around to doin' it. Now Great-granny was gone and Great-grandpa was left on his own—an old man.

I wondered what other thoughts were scurryin' through my grandpa's mind. A movement beside me made me lift my head. Grandpa reached over and placed his hand on my knee. I was surprised to see tears in his eyes. His voice was a bit husky as he spoke.

"Boy," he said, "you and me have another thing in common now—the hurt of havin' no ma."

He gave my knee a squeeze. As the words that he'd jest said sank in, I swallowed hard.

He started talkin' then. I had rarely heard my Grandpa talk so much at one time—unless it was a neighbor-visit or a discussion with Uncle Charlie.

"Funny how many memories come stealin' back fresh as if they'd jest happened. Haven't thought on them fer years, but they're still there fer jest sech a time."

He was silent a moment, deep in thought.

"Yer great-granny weren't much of a woman far as size goes, but what she lacked in stature she made up for in spunk." He chuckled. It seemed strange to hear him laugh and see tears layin' on his tanned and weathered cheeks.

"I was 'bout five at the time. There was an old tree in a vacant lot near our house, and it was my favorite climbin' tree. I was up there livin' in my own world of make-believe when the neighborhood dogs came around and started playin' around the tree. I didn't pay 'em any mind until I was hot and thirsty and decided I'd had enough play. I started to crawl down, but a big black mutt I'd never seen before spotted me and wouldn't let me out of that tree.

"I yelled and bawled until I was hoarse, but I was too far

away to be heard at the house. Mama—" when that one word slipped out so easily I knew that Grandpa was truly back relivin' the boyhood experience again—"she waited my dinner fer me and fussed that I was late again. But as time went on and I still didn't come, her worry drove her out lookin' fer me.

"When she caught sight of the tree, she spied the mutt standin' guard at that tree and figured out jest what was goin' on. She grabbed a baseball bat lyin' in a neighbor's yard and came a-marchin' down. I can see her yet—that little bit of a woman with her club fairly blazin', she was so mad! Well, that mutt soon learned that he was no match fer my mama. Never did see that dog again."

Grandpa chuckled again.

"Funny how a woman can be bold as an army when there's a need fer it, and yet so gentle. Yer great-granny was one of the kindest, gentlest people I ever knew. Jest the touch of her hand brushed the fever from ya. And when she gathered ya into her arms in her old rockin' chair after she had washed ya all up fer bed, and held ya close against her, and rocked back and forth hummin' an old hymn and kissin' yer hair . . . "

Grandpa stopped and swallowed and another tear slid down his cheek.

"Shucks," he said, "I knew that I was too old fer that, but as long as the neighbor kids didn't catch me at it. . . Funny how loved I felt."

"Then one day I knew that I was jest too big to be hugged and rocked anymore—but I missed it, and I think Mama did, too. I often caught that longin' look in her eye. She'd reach fer me, and I thought that she was goin' to pull me into her lap again. Then instead, her hand would scoot to my head and she'd tousle my hair and scold me fer my dirty feet or torn overalls."

Grandpa had forgotten all about the team that he was supposed to be drivin', and the horses were takin' every advantage given them. No horse could have gone any slower and still have been puttin' one foot in front of the other. Old Bell, who always insisted on havin' her own way, drew as far to her side of the road—which happened to be the wrong side—as she dared. Every now and then she would reach down and steal a mouthful of grass without really stoppin' to graze. Nellie didn't particularly seem to mind goin' slowly either.

I watched the horses and glanced back at Grandpa, wondering jest how long he was going to put up with the situation. I think he had even forgotten *me*.

He stopped talkin' but I could tell by the different expressions on his face that his mind was still mullin' over old memories. Many of them had been happy memories, but they brought sadness now that they were never to be again.

Suddenly Grandpa roused himself and turned to me.

"Memories are beautiful things, Boy. When the person that ya loved is gone, when the happy time is over, then ya've still got yer memories. Thank God fer this special gift of His that lets ya sorta live yer experiences again and again. S'pose there ain't no price one would settle on fer the worth of memories."

A new thought washed over me, makin' me feel all at once cheated, frustrated, and angry. I was sure that Grandpa was right. I had never thought about memories much before; but deep down inside me there would sometimes awaken a somethin' that seemed groping, looking, reaching out for feelings or answers that were beyond me. It seemed to me now that Grandpa had somehow put his finger on it for me. He had said when he read his letter that he and I shared the loss of our mothers. That was true. But even as he said it I knew somehow there was a difference. As I heard him talk, it suddenly hit me what the difference was; it was the memories—or for me, the lack of them. Grandpa could go on and on about things he recalled from his childhood: his mother's face, her smile, her smell, her touch. Me, all I had was a great big blank spot—only a name—"You had a mother, Boy, her name was Agatha. Pretty name, Agatha."

Sometimes I laid awake at night tryin' to put a face to that name, but I never could. When I was younger I'd watch the faces of ladies, and when I found one that I liked, I'd pretend that was the way my mother's face had looked. One time I went for almost two years pretendin' about the banker's wife in town; then I realized how foolish I was and made myself stop playin' the silly game. And now Grandpa sat there thankin' God for memories.

A sick feelin' began to knot up my stomach and I felt a little angry with God. Why did He think it fair to take my parents when I was only a baby and not even leave me with memories like other folks? Wasn't it bad enough to be a kid without a mom to hug him or a pa to go fishin' with him?

I didn't dare look at Grandpa. I was afraid that he'd look right through me and see the ugly feelings inside. I looked instead at the horses. Old Bell grabbed another mouthful of grass, but this time she made the mistake of stoppin' to snatch a second bite from the same clump. Nellie sort of jerked the harness because she was still movin'—if you could call it that. Anyway, the whole thing brought Grandpa out of his remembering, and his attention swung back to the horses. He could hardly believe his eyes. He'd never allowed a team such liberties. His hands yanked the slack from the reins, and Bell felt a smack on her round gray rump which startled her so that she dropped her last mouthful of grass. Soon the team was back on its proper side of the road and hustling along at a trot.

Grandpa turned to me with a foolish-lookin' grin.

"If we don't hurry some, we'll be late fer dinner and Lou will have both of our heads."

I grinned back rather weakly, for I was still feelin' sort of mad that I'd been badly cheated in life. Besides, we both knew that what he'd said wasn't true. Auntie Lou didn't make much fuss at all when we were late for a meal. Maybe that's why all three of us—Grandpa, Uncle Charlie and me—always tried not to keep her waitin'. I guess we all counted Auntie Lou as someone pretty special. And without really thinkin' about it, we each tried hard to keep things from being any tougher for her than they needed to be.

Chapter 2

Changes

As was often his habit after our evening meal, Grandpa had me fetch his Bible so's we could have what he called "family worship time." I generally found it sort of borin', listenin' to all that stuff about "The Lord is my shepherd," and other things that people wrote way back in ancient times.

Grandpa's mood seemed to be a little different that night while he read. I guess it was because of the letter from his pa. Anyway, it made me feel a bit strange, too, to see him feelin' that way.

The letter that Grandpa received was jest the first of the things to start causin' me to feel a little uneasiness about life—the life of one, Joshua Chadwick Jones in particular. The next upsetting thing happened that night after I had been sent to bed.

Now I knew that my bedtime was s'posed to be at nine, but I never did go up when the clock said the time had arrived. I'd wait first to hear Grandpa say, "Bedtime, Boy," then I'd wash myself in the basin by the door and slowly climb the stairs to my room.

I always kinda figured that maybe some night Grandpa would become occupied with something and forget to watch the clock, but it never happened.

Tonight Grandpa's mind was busy elsewhere, I could tell that. He had read the letter to Auntie Lou and Uncle Charlie. Auntie Lou had put her arms around each of them and given them a warm hug as the tears formed in her eyes. Uncle Charlie hadn't said much, but I was sure that he was busy sortin' memories jest as Grandpa had done, and I felt a tug at my stomach again.

As the hands of the clock crawled toward nine, I waited. If ever Grandpa was goin' to miss his cue, tonight would be the night. But he didn't. Promptly at nine he said, "Boy, it's yer bedtime." I let out a long sigh. I had been prepared to steal a little extra time like Bell had stolen the extra mouthfuls of summer grass—but it hadn't worked.

I went through my usual routine. As I headed for the stairs I heard Auntie Lou say, "I think I'll go up now, too, Pa." She leaned over and kissed Grandpa on the cheek. "Good-night, Uncle Charlie." He nodded at her and Lou and I climbed the stairs together. As we climbed she let her hand rest on my shoulder.

"Won't be long," she said, "until I'll have to reach *up* to put my hand on yer shoulder. Yer really growin', Josh. Look at those overalls—short again!"

Auntie Lou made it sound like a real accomplishment to outgrow overalls, and I jest grinned.

" 'Night Josh."

" 'Night."

I settled into bed but I couldn't get to sleep. I lay there twistin' and turnin', and inside I seemed to be twistin' and turnin', too. Finally I decided that a drink of water might help. Grandpa didn't take too kindly to a boy using the drink excuse too often, but I reckoned that jest this once I oughta be able to get away with it.

My room was the first one at the top of the stairs that came up from the kitchen. I knew that Grandpa and Uncle Charlie would be sitting at the kitchen table having a last cup of coffee before bed and talking over anything that needed talking over, or jest sitting there in companionable silence. I put on my most innocent little-boy expression and started down the stairs. A voice from below stopped me short.

" . . . it's the only thing that can be done as fer as I can see." It was Grandpa talkin'.

I heard a sucking noise. I knew what it was. Folks 'round about said that Uncle Charlie could down a cup of coffee hotter and quicker than any other man they knew. Not too much distinction for a man, but at least it was something, and I often took to watchin' Uncle Charlie empty his cup, mentally figurin' if he might have broken his own record. Before Uncle Charlie would take a swallow of the scalding liquid, he would sorta suck in air with a funny whistlin' sound. I s'pose the mouthful of air served to cool the coffee some on its way down, I don't know.

I heard that sound now and I could almost see the steaming cup leaning against Uncle Charlie's lips. He'd be sittin' there with his chair tilted back slightly, restin' on only the back two legs. This was hard on chairs, I was told when I tried to copy Uncle Charlie, but nobody ever scolded Uncle Charlie for it.

There came the sound of the cup being replaced on the table and then the gentle thump of the two front legs of the chair joinin' the back two on the hardwood kitchen floor.

"Do ya think he'll agree to it?"

"I don't know. He's so stubborn 'n' independent. You remember that as well as I do. But now, maybe he'd welcome the change. He's gonna be powerful lonely. Ya know what she was to him."

By now I had changed my mind about the drink of water and settled myself quietly on the step. I could feel a shiver go through my whole body. Things were changin'. I didn't know why and I didn't know how it was going to affect me, but I wasn't welcomin' it.

"Well, we've at least gotta try. We can't jest let him stay there alone. I'll go to town tomorrow and call him on Kirk's tellyphone. It'll take him awhile to sort things out, but I really would like him to come and stay. Lots of room here. No reason at all that he can't move right in."

"S'pose."

I knew that they must be talking about Great-grandpa. Why, he was an old man. I had watched the old men in town shufflin' their way down the street, lookin' weak-kneed and watery-eyed. Sometimes three or four of them gathered on the bench outside the livery stable and jest sat and talked and chewed tobacco that dribbled down their old quivery chins and stained their shirt fronts. I don't suppose I could have put it into words, but I didn't like the idea of an old man coming here—even if he was my great-grandpa. I didn't want to hear anymore, but I couldn't pull myself away.

"Something seems to bother ya," Grandpa said to Uncle Charlie. "Don't ya agree that Pa should come?"

Uncle Charlie stirred himself.

"Well, he's got to be looked after, that's fer sure, and I'm—well, I'd be right happy to see him. It's been a long time, but I was wonderin'—maybe—maybe I should go on back East and sorta care fer him there."

Grandpa seemed surprised at Uncle Charlie's suggestion; I knew that I was. I jest couldn't imagine life without Uncle Charlie.

"You wantin' to go back East?" Grandpa exclaimed.

"Lan' sakes no." Uncle Charlie's reply was rather loud, as though Grandpa was kinda dull to even think that such a thing could be possible.

"Ya thinkin' Pa couldn't make the trip?"

"By the way his letter reads he's still sound enough."

"Then what—"

"Lou."

"Lou?"

"Yeah, Lou."

"Lou wouldn't object."

"No, she wouldn't. That's jest the point—she should."

"I'm afraid I don't follow."

"Daniel, how many other seventeen-year-old girls do ya know who care fer a big house, a garden, chickens, two old men, and a boy?"

There was silence for a while and then Uncle Charlie spoke again.

"And now we want to saddle her with another old man. Ain't fair—jest ain't fair. She should be out partyin' and—"

Grandpa cut in. "Lou ain't much fer partyin'."

" 'Course she ain't. She's never had a chance. We've kept her bakin' bread and scrubbin' floors ever since she laid her dolls aside."

Silence again. Grandpa broke it.

"Ya think Lou's unhappy?"

" 'Course she's happy!" snorted Uncle Charlie. "She's too unselfish *not* to be happy. She knows if she wasn't happy we'd all be miser'ble. Lou wouldn't do that to anyone."

Grandpa sighed deeply, like an old wound was suddenly painin' him. He roused and I could hear him rattlin' around with the coffeepot. Now I knew that he was agitated. Grandpa never, never drank more than one cup of coffee before bed, but I heard him pour them each another cup now.

"Yer right," he finally said; "it's been tough fer Lou."

"What'll happen is, she'll go right from keepin' this house to keepin' someone else's." A slight pause. "And that might happen 'fore we know it, too."

"Lou? Why she's jest a kid!"

"Kid nothin'! She's reachin' fer eighteen. Her ma was married at that age iffen you'll remember, and so was her grandma."

"Never thought of Lou—"

"Other people been thinkin'. Everytime we go to town, be it fer business or church, I see those young whipper-snappers eyin' her and tryin' to tease a smile or a nod from her. One of these days she's gonna notice it, too."

Grandpa stirred uneasily in his chair.

"She's pretty."

" 'Course she's pretty—those big blue eyes and that smile. Why iffen I was a young fella, I'd never be a hangin' back like I see those fellas doin'."

Uncle Charlie had barely finished his sentence when Grandpa's fist came down hard on the table.

"Confound it, Charlie, we been sleepin'. Here's Lou sneak-in' right up there to marryin' age, and we ain't even been workin' on it."

"And what ya figurin' *we* git to do 'bout it?"

"Like ya say, it's gonna happen, and it could be soon. We gotta git busy lookin' fer someone fittin' fer Lou. I ain't gonna give my little girl away to jest any starry-eyed young joe who happens to come along."

"Don't ya trust Lou?"

"Look! Ya know and I know that she can't see evil in a skunk! Now iffen the wrong guy should start payin' calls, how is a young innocent girl like Lou gonna know what's really under that fancy shirt? You and I, Charlie, we've been around some. We know the kind a fella that would be good fer Lou. We've jest gotta step in there and see to it that Lou meets the right one."

"How we gonna manage that?"

"I don't know 'xactly; we gotta find a way. Git a piece of paper, Charlie, and I'll find a pencil."

"Fer what?"

"We gotta do some thinkin' and make a list. We don't wanna be caught off-guard."

Uncle Charlie grumbled but I heard him tear a spent month from the calendar on the kitchen wall and return to the table.

"Let's be systematic 'bout this," said Grandpa. "We'll work to the south first, then west, then north, then to the east, includin' town.

"First there's Wilkins—no grown boys there. The Petersons—all girls. Turleys—s'pose that oldest one must be gittin' nigh to twenty, but he's so shy."

"Lazy too—never lifts a hand if he doesn't have to."

"Put him on the re-ject side."

The pencil scratched on the paper, and I could picture Jake Turley's name bein' entered on the back side of the calendar sheet under "rejected."

"Crawfords—there's two there: Eb and Sandy."

"Eb's got a girl."

Again the pencil scratched and another candidate was eliminated.

"Sandy?"

"He's 'bout as bullheaded as—"

"Scratch 'im."

"Haydon?"

"There's Milt."

"What do ya think 'bout Milt?"

"He's a good worker."

"Not too good lookin'."

"Looks ain't everything."

"Hope Lou knows that."

"He wouldn't be so bad if it wasn't fer his crooked teeth."

"Lou's teeth are so nice and even."

"S'pose all their kids would have crooked teeth like their pa."

I heard the pencil at work again and I didn't even have to wonder what side Milt's name was bein' written on. By now I'd had enough. Jest as I pulled my achin' self up from the step and was about to turn back up to bed, I heard Uncle Charlie speak again.

"We still haven't settled 'bout Pa."

"No problem now," said Grandpa. "It'll take him awhile to git here and with Lou married and settled on her own, she won't need to be carin' fer three old men. We can batch. We've done it before."

Uncle Charlie grunted, "Yeah, guess so." They went on to the next neighbor and I went back up the stairs.

A sick feelin' in my stomach was spreadin' all through me. We were an unusual family, I knew that, but we belonged together. We fit somehow, and I guess I was foolish enough to somehow believe that things would always stay that way. Suddenly, with no warnin', everything was now about to change. Jest like that, I was to trade Auntie Lou for an old tottery great-grandfather that I had never seen. It sure didn't seem like much of a trade.

I started going to my room and then changed my mind. I couldn't resist going on down the hall to the end room where Auntie Lou slept. I paused at her door which was open just a crack. I could hear her soft breathin'. I pushed the door gently and eased myself into the room. The moon cast enough light through the window so that I could see clearly Auntie Lou's face. She *was* pretty! I had never thought about it before. I had never stopped to ask the question nor to look for the answer. She was Auntie Lou. She was jest always there. I'd never had to decide what she was to me. Now that I might be losing her I realized that she was *everything*—the mother I'd never known, a big sister, a playmate, my best friend. Auntie Lou was all of these and more, wrapped up in one neat little five-foot-three package.

I swallowed the lump in my throat, but I couldn't keep the tears from runnin' down my cheeks. I brushed them away feelin' angry with myself.

There she slept, so peaceful-like, while downstairs two old men were deciding who she would spend the rest of her life with; and Lou was so easy goin' that they'd likely get away with it. Unless. . .

I backed slowly out of the door and tip-toed to my room, makin' sure I missed the spot that always squeaked. Down below the voices droned on. I shut my door tight against them and crawled back under the covers. I realized suddenly jest how tired I was. I pulled the blankets right up to my chin.

Somehow there had to be a way I could stop this. Somehow! It wasn't gonna be easy; it was gonna take a lot of thinkin', but surely if I worked it over in my mind enough I'd find some way.

My thoughts began to get foggy as I fought sleep. I'd have to figure it all out later. Then a new idea flashed through my mind—prayer. I'd already said my evenin' prayers as Auntie Lou had taught me, but this one was extra. I'm not sure jest what I asked from God in my sleepy state, but I think that it went something like this:

"Dear God. You know what they're plannin' fer Auntie Lou, but I want to keep her. You didn't let me keep my ma—or my pa. You didn't even give me any memories. Now you gotta help me to find a way to stop this.

"And about Great-grandpa—maybe you could find him a new wife, even if he is old, so that he won't need to come here. Or maybe he could die on the train comin' out or somethin'.

Anyway, please do what you can, God. You sorta owe me a favor after all you've taken from me. Amen."

Satisfied that I had done what I could for the time bein,' I crawled back into bed. I wasn't sure that God would pay too much attention to my prayer, but anyway, I'd tried. Tomorrow I'd work on a plan so that I'd be ready on my own if God decided not to do anything for me.

I went to sleep with the voices from the kitchen risin' and fallin' as the two men sorted through their lists. I wondered if they had come up with anyone for the accepted side of the page yet. Then I rolled over and went to sleep.

Chapter 3

About Lou

That had all taken place yesterday. Somehow as I sat on my log it seemed long ago and hardly even real, yet at the same time, present and frightenin'. I had to worry it through and find a solution.

Again, as I had in times past, I wished that I had a dog. Somehow it seemed that jest the presence of *something* with me would make the whole thing easier to handle. Well, I *didn't* have a dog, so I'd jest have to find an answer on my own.

Before, I had always been able to go to Auntie Lou with the things that bothered me, but I knew this was one problem that I couldn't discuss with her. On the one hand, I found myself achin' to tell her so that she would be warned; on the other hand, I knew that I would do all that I could to hide the ugly facts from her—to protect her from knowin'.

Guess I should explain a bit about Auntie Lou and why she is only five years older than me. Grandpa had met and fallen in love with my grandma, a bubbly wisp of a girl. They married young and went farmin'. A year later they had a baby boy whom everyone said was a combination of the two of them. He had the colorin' and the size of my grandpa who was a big man, but the disposition and looks of my grandma.

When my pa, who they named Chadwick, was three years old, Grandma was stricken with some awful illness. I never did hear a name put to it, but she was dreadfully sick and the baby that she was expectin' was born only to die two days later. Grandpa and the doctor were so busy fightin' to save my grandma that the loss of the baby didn't really hit them until Grandma came 'round enough to start askin' for her. She had wanted that baby girl so much and she cried buckets over losin' her. For days she grieved and cried for her baby. The doctor feared that she would jest sorrow herself right into her grave, so he had a talk with Grandpa.

The next day Grandpa washed and combed my pa and dressed him in his fanciest clothes. Then he lifted the little fella up in his arms and they paid a call to Grandma's bedside. Grandpa never did say what words were spoken as he and the boy stood there by the bed, but Grandma got the message and from then on she laid aside her sorrow and determined to get well again.

It was a long uphill pull, but she made it—by sheer willpower many said. But never again was she strong enough to be the bouncy young woman that my grandpa had married. He accepted her as she was and gradually talked and loved her into accepting herself as well. She finally agreed that rest periods must now be a part of her daily schedule, but it took awhile to adjust to her new way of life.

The years slipped quickly by. My pa grew to be a lanky kid, then a young man. But all the while, though her eyes glowed with pride over her son, deep down in her heart Grandma still yearned for a baby girl. Finally she admitted, "If the Lord wills, I still wish to be blessed with a daughter before I leave this old world." My pa was twenty when his baby sister arrived. Grandma was beside herself with joy. She named the wee baby Louisa Jennifer, the Jennifer bein' her own name.

Even though her prayer had been answered—her dream fulfilled—Grandma never regained her strength. Most of the fussin' over her new baby had to be done upon her own bed, she bein' only strong enough to be up for short periods of time. She smothered love on my Auntie Lou. Grandpa often said that Auntie Lou had no choice but to be lovin' when she had love piled on her in such big batches.

Lou was only two when Grandma's condition worsened. Chad, my pa, was about to go farmin' on his own, havin' met and married a certain sweet young gal by the name of Agatha Creycroft—my ma. That's when Uncle Charlie was sent for. He came gladly and has been with us ever since.

The next winter Grandma passed away and the two men, a father, more up in years than most fathers, and a bachelor uncle, were left to raise a little girl not yet turned three.

She was a bright, happy little sprite. Grandma always declared that God sure knew what He was doin' when He saw fit to answer my grandma's prayer. Lou was their sunshine, their joy, the center of their attention. Odd, with all of the love and attention she got that she didn't spoil, but she didn't. She grew up jest as ready to love and accept others.

Then I came along. My folks were farmin' only four miles away from my grandpa's home place. I was jest big enough to smile and coo when both my folks were killed in an accident on their farm. Again the two men had a child to raise, but this time they had help. The five-year-old Lou sorta claimed me right from the start. I can't remember any further back than to Lou—this strange woman-child whose pixie face leaned over my crib or hushed me when I fussed. We grew up together. She was both parent and playmate to me. The parents that I never knew really weren't missed—except when I would purposely set my mind to wonderin'. Usually, as my childhood days ticked by I was happy and content. When Lou needed to go to school, I stayed with Grandpa or Uncle Charlie, chafin' for her return in the afternoon. She would run most of the way home and then she would scoop me into her arms. "Oh, Joshie sweetheart," or, "My little darlin'," she'd say, then ask, "Did ya miss me, honey? Come on, let's go play"; and we would, while Grandpa got the evenin' meal and Uncle Charlie did the chores.

At last the day arrived when I placed my hand in Auntie Lou's, and sharin' a pail filled with our lunch, we went off to school together. Those were good years. The two men home on the farm enjoyed a freedom that they hadn't had for years, and I never had to be separated from Lou.

Grandpa held fast to the rules of proper respect, so at home I always addressed her as Auntie Lou. But at school we conspired to make it jest Lou, in order not to be teased by the other kids.

The school years went well. I was a fair student and anytime that I did hit a snag, I had special coachin' from Lou who was always near the head of her class.

As we grew up, Grandpa assigned us responsibilities; Lou took on more and more of the housework, and I began to help with outside chores. Still we used all of the minutes that we could find to play together. I would, with some convincing, pick flowers with Lou in exchange for her carryin' the pail while we hunted frogs. Often she didn' jest carry—she caught as many frogs as I did. She could shinny up a tree as fast as any boy, too, tuckin' her skirt in around her elastic bloomer legs in order to get it out of her way. She could also skip rocks and throw a ball.

She would take a dare to walk the skinniest rail on the fence and outdo any fella at school. Yet somehow when she hopped to the ground and assumed her role as "girl," she could be as proper and appealin' as could be, and could give you that look of pure innocence fittin' for a princess or an angel.

Lou completed the grades in the local school, and then it was me who went off alone each mornin'. She stayed behind, responsible now for managin' the house and feedin' two hungry men and a growing boy.

It was my turn to run home at day's end, knowing that if I hurried there would still be a few minutes of fun before chore time. We still knew how to make the most of the minutes that we had. We took quick trips to the crik where we laid on our stomachs and startled minnows or worried turtles. We visited the pond where we skipped rocks or turned over stones to see who could win by findin' the highest number of insects underneath. We hunted bird nests, being careful not to disturb the inhabitants. We played on the haystacks, makin' ourselves a slide that was a bit hard on the clothes, but great fun regardless. On colder days we'd tell a story or play a game—or jest talk.

All of the time that I was growin' up with Auntie Lou, I had never stopped to consider what kind of a human being she was. She was jest there; she was necessary, she was mine, and now, now all of a sudden, I was forced to realize that she was a girl—a girl almost a woman, a girl who might marry and move away to live with some man. Again anger swept through me. I hated him—this other man whoever he would be; I hated him. Somehow I planned to stop this awful thing from happenin' if I could. I still hadn't figured out how I'd do it, but I'd take 'em as they came, one by one, and I'd git rid of 'em. They'd all be on the reject list.

I pushed my toes down deeper into the mud. The water gurgled about my legs. A small turtle poked his head above the water's surface beside the log, and I reached down angrily and pushed him under again. I hadn't hurt him, I knew that, but somehow I felt a tiny bit better gettin' a chance to spend some of the meanness I was feelin'.

I heard a soft step on the trail behind me and knew without havin' to look that it was Auntie Lou. Only she walked like that—gently and quickly. I didn't even turn my head but busied myself tryin' to get my face back to what she was used to seeing so that she wouldn't start askin' questions. I heard her slip her shoes off and then she stepped to the log. Her hand rested on my shoulder for balance as she carefully sat down beside me and stretched her feet into the water.

We said nothin'—jest sat there swishin' our feet back and forth. She tucked her skirts up so that the hems wouldn't reach the water. She seemed to settle in for a long stay.

"Hungry?"

All of a sudden it hit me. Boy, was I hungry! I glanced up at the sky and was shocked at where the sun hung. It must've been past time for lunch. I should have been to table ages ago. I supposed she'd waited and waited. I started to stammer an apology or an excuse; I wasn't sure which it was going to be, but Auntie Lou interrupted me.

"Brought some lunch."

Then I spied our old lunch pail in her hand.

"Pa and Uncle Charlie went to town. They want to git in touch with Grandpa right away. They're gonna try to telephone him. Doesn't it seem funny to be able to talk with someone hundreds of miles away? If they can't git him by phone, they'll send a telegram."

As Auntie Lou talked she removed the lid and passed the pail to me to help myself to the sandwiches. I fairly drooled.

"Boy," I said, avoiding the Great-grandpa issue, "never realized how hungry I was. Good thing that ya came along or I might've starved right here and slipped into the crik, stone dead."

Auntie Lou giggled softly as though what I had said was really clever.

"Good thing that I saved the turtles and the fish from the disaster."

We ate in silence for a while. Finally Lou broke it.

"Did ya know that Pa is goin' to ask Grandpa to come out here to live, now that Grandma is gone?"

I nodded my head, hopin' that she wouldn't ask me where I'd gathered the knowledge. She didn't.

"What do *you* think?" I finally asked.

"About Grandpa comin'?"

"Yeah."

I pulled out another sandwich.

"I hope he does. What do *you* think?" Lou returned the question.

I hunched my shoulders carelessly.

"Don't know. Doesn't matter to me much I guess. It's you that'll have to wash his clothes and get his meals and care fer 'im iffen he's too old to care fer himself."

"He'll care fer himself."

I turned toward her. My voice sounded sharp and impatient. "He's an old man, Lou—an old man. He's *my great-grandpa*. He could be yer great-grandpa, too, as far as years go. We don't know; he could be drooly or half-blind or all crippled up with arthritis or anything!"

Lou's answer was typically Lou.

"If he is—then he needs us even more."

I turned back to the water and kicked my feet harder. Lou wasn't going to see it. She didn't want to see it. She was going to let them bring him out here—that old man. Then the only way she would be freed from the burden of carin' for him would be to marry some young fella and move away. I kicked again.

"Yer pant legs are all wet, Josh." She said it softly, matter-of-factly, but I knew that what she really meant was that my pant legs had no business being wet.

"Sorry," I mumbled and squirmed back farther onto the log so that my legs didn't reach as deeply into the water.

She didn't comment further but jest passed me the cookies and an apple.

"Are ya worried, Josh?"

"Worried?"

"Yeah, that Grandpa might not fit in or like us or something?"

The last thing that I was worried about was whether Great-grandpa would like us or not, but I didn't say that to Auntie Lou. I shrugged.

Auntie Lou took a delicate bite from her apple.

"Don't think that ya need to worry none. Pa has told me some things about him. I think that we'll git along jest fine."

"Maybe," I said, not committing myself.

Lou put the lid back on the pail.

"Well, I'd best git back to the house. Still haven't finished the washin'—jest the socks left. Ugh! I hate scrubbin' socks."

She screwed up her face, then laughed at her own teasin'. *Sure*, I thought, *you hate scrubbing socks and here ya are askin' for some more.* But I didn't say it.

"Pa said that you should hoe another row or two of potatoes this afternoon."

I started up from the log, knowin' that if those potatoes were going to get done, I'd better get at them. Lou put on her shoes and we started off toward the house together, her shoes and my bare feet leaving side-by-side prints in the dust of the path. She hummed as she walked and swung the pail playfully in large sweeps.

"Lou?"

"Yeah."

I hesitated. "Oh, skip it," I finally said.

She looked at me, her big blue eyes looking serious and even bluer.

"Go ahead," she said. "If ya have something to say, say it."

"Are you plannin' on gittin' married?" She stopped short and looked sharply at me like I'd lost my senses.

"Me?" She pointed a finger at herself.

"Yeah."

"Whatever made ya ask somethin' like that? Why I—I ain't even got a beau." She blushed slightly.

"Well, I don't mean tomorrow or nothin' like that—but someday?"

"Someday?" She thought a bit and chuckled then. "Oh, Josh, ya dumbhead." She ruffled my mop of hair. "Yeah, I s'pose. Maybe someday I'll git married."

Fear grabbed at my throat. She seemed to like the idea by the light in her eyes. Then she hurried on.

"Someday, maybe, but not fer a long, long time."

I could feel the air comin' back into my lungs.

"Ya sure?"

"I'm sure. Why, I haven't even given it any serious thought. And I sure am not ready to take on another man and another house jest now."

"Yet you'd take on Great-grandpa?"

"That's different," said Lou. She sounded so certain that I was prepared to believe her. "Grandpa is *ours* and he will be in the same house. It scarce will make any difference at all."

I wanted to believe her. With all of my heart I wanted to believe her. If it was like she said and Great-grandpa fit into the house, and the family, and everything worked out well, maybe Grandpa and Uncle Charlie would soon realize that they wouldn't have to marry Auntie Lou off after all. Maybe it *could* work out. I still didn't welcome the idea of the old man comin', but I no longer felt such a knot of fear tearin' at my insides.

Chapter 4

Correction

Feelin' a little better after my talk with Auntie Lou, I set to work on the potato patch with real determination. By the time I heard the team returning from town with Grandpa and Uncle Charlie, I was on my fourth row. Uncle Charlie took the horses on down to the barn, and Grandpa came out to the garden to see me. He was right pleased with what I had accomplished. I puffed with pride a bit.

"I think you've worked long enough in the hot sun, Boy. Best leave the rest for tomorrow. Let's go see if yer Auntie Lou has somethin' cold to drink."

Uncle Charlie fell in step beside us as we headed for the house. I didn't ask the question that I was dying to ask. I knew that it would all be laid out before us at the time of Grandpa's choosin'.

Lou had some cold milk and man-sized sugar cookies sitting on the table. We three sat down after washing our hands at the washbasin and drying them briskly on the rough towel.

I looked at Lou; I could see that she wasn't goin' to wait long for details on what happened in town. If Grandpa didn't soon volunteer the information, she'd start askin' questions.

Grandpa took a long drink of his milk. Lou had enough patience to let him swallow.

"Did you reach him?"

Lou didn't play little games of beat-around-the-bush. She was always honest and direct. So was Grandpa.

"Yeah, we did. Had to make two calls on the tellyphone. Some contraption, that. Couldn't believe my ears. Here I was a-talkin' to my own pa hundreds of miles away. A few years ago iffen someone had said that sech a thing would be possible, they'd laughed him out of town."

"Or locked him up," Uncle Charlie suggested.

"Why *two* calls?" asked Auntie Lou.

"First time he wasn't in."

Lou was gettin' real impatient by now.

"But you did get to talk to him?" She prodded.

"We sure did—both of us. He could hardly believe it. Said it made him so lonesome that he felt like jest hoppin' a westbound train."

There was a moment's silence as Grandpa sat there lookin' down at his milk glass. Uncle Charlie was lookin' down, too, as he twisted his glass 'round and 'round in his big fingers.

"Does he plan to come?"

Both Lou and I seemed to be holdin' our breath. Grandpa looked up.

"Yeah, he'll come! He's missin' Ma something awful. He'll come! It'll take him awhile to get everything all cared for, but it shouldn't be too long; then he'll be out—by harvest time for sure."

"Did he—did he sound. . . ?" I knew that my question wasn't coming out right. I wanted to know if Great-grandpa sounded like he still had all of his senses in spite of his age, but I didn't want Grandpa and Uncle Charlie—or Auntie Lou—to figure out what I wanted to know. I wished, as I stammered around, that I had never opened my mouth. Uncle Charlie seemed to realize that I was squirmin' like a bug on a hot rock.

"Sounded good—real good. Voice still strong and steady. Talked of his garden!"

Uncle Charlie's eyes took on a twinkle.

"S'pose he out-hoed you today, Josh—and you figure that you had a pretty good day!"

I squirmed a bit more and reached for another cookie, more or less jest for something to do. In spite of my embarrassment I was glad now that I had asked the question. I had heard what I'd wanted to hear—about the old man's health, that is, not about his plans for a train-trip west. I still felt mighty uneasy about that. Still, it was only midsummer, and anything could happen between now and harvest time—well anyway, almost anything.

"Iffen you'll excuse me," I said, "I think I'll be finishin' that row before chore time."

I could feel three pairs of eyes on my back as I left the kitchen, and I knew that they must all be wonderin' iffen I'd had too much sun. I had never laid claim to enjoying hoein', and truth was, I didn't care much for it now; but it was the only excuse that I could come up with for gettin' away from the table. I knew very well that the three of them were gonna go on talkin' about Great-grandpa; and as they talked their faces and their voices showed that they were all excited about his soon comin'. The fact that I didn't share their enthusiasm made me feel kinda mean-like. Yet there was no way that I knew of to change the way I was feelin'; so I chose to get me out to where there was no one to search me out.

I finished the row in record time and still had a few minutes to kill before I needed to start on the chores. I decided to take a walk to the pond to check on the ducks that had nested there.

The mother had hatched seven ducklings and already their feathers had changed. Every time I saw them they had grown some.

They didn't seem to mind me around as long as I didn't try to get too close. I would sit on the shore, my back against a big ol' tree and watch their funnin' around as long as I wanted to.

For some reason they failed to amuse me today. Guess my mind was too heavy with other things. Lou certainly hadn't seemed upset to hear that Great-grandpa was plannin' to come. In fact, she had looked pleased and excited about it. Whether she really meant it or was just tryin' to please Grandpa and Uncle Charlie, I wasn't sure. If she really did mean it and didn't mind takin' on another family member, even if it was an old man, maybe I could relax again. I sure did feel mixed up. It wasn't until I had been threatened with losing Auntie Lou that I realized just how important she was to me.

I was headin' back toward the barn when I remembered about my prayin' the night before. Maybe God did choose to answer a kid's prayer. Jest as I started to feel kinda good about it, I remembered other parts of my prayer. If God really took me seriously, then I had the feelin' that He didn't care much for some of what I'd been askin' for. My conscience started a-prickin' at me, and I realized that if I wanted any peace, I had some correctin' to do. I stepped off the path into the trees and knelt down.

"Dear God," I said, "I wanta thank ya for spendin' yer time and energy working on my prayer.

"Please, can ya jest forget that part 'bout havin' him die on the train? It's okay if he comes—I guess.

"And don't bother 'bout a new wife. He'd jest bring her, too, and we sure don't need that. Thank ya. Amen."

I felt a little better then. I wasn't sure if it was God that I feared or my family—should they ever find out that I had brought down fire from heaven on a man they loved and wanted. Anyway, God and I had it sorted out now, so there wasn't much need to worry over it any longer.

I headed for the granary to get the feed for the pigs, pretendin', as I often did, that I had my own dog runnin' beside me.

Today he was small and black with a splash of white on his chest, and droopy ears. His coat was curly and his tail fluffed over his back. I named him Shadow because of the way he stuck with me. As I went about the chores, I'd scold him for barkin' at the pigs, then I'd sic him on the big red bull. He'd pull on my pant legs and nearly trip me by crowdin' in close to me. I'd try to quiet him down as we fed the chickens.

Grandpa might have frowned on the game had he known,

but it sure helped the chorin' to be a lot more fun. I couldn't help but think how it would be if Shadow was a real live dog. I had hinted once or twice that it would sure be useful to have a good dog about the farm, but Grandpa didn't seem to catch on. He once had a dog that he thought an awful lot of. Lived to be fifteen years old, which is awfully old for a dog. Seemed like when he died, Grandpa jest never had the heart to get him another dog. Wasn't that he didn't like dogs; he jest hadn't considered fillin' the gap that his old comrade had left. I didn't want to bring sadness to Grandpa, so I didn't go beyond the hints. Still, I sure did wish that I had me my own dog.

Chapter 5

Uneasy Again

The summer was goin' along nice and smooth. The hayin' was all done and the crops were lookin' good. I had pushed all thoughts of impendin' doom from my mind. I was feelin' like my world would continue on as it was for jest as long as I wanted it to—which would prob'ly be forever—when Grandpa hit me with a real knock-downer.

Now if I hadn't heard the conversation that night on the kitchen stairs, I wouldn't have paid any attention to what Grandpa said now.

We were riding home from church on a hot Sunday. It would have been too hot if it hadn't been for a breeze that was blowin'. I was sitting at the back of the wagon hanging my bare feet down so that they could swing; I'd taken off my Sunday shoes and my socks as soon as we were a respectable distance from the church. Then I heard Grandpa speak to Auntie Lou.

At Grandpa's words my mind snapped to attention. I had been feelin' pretty secure thinkin' that Grandpa and Uncle Charlie had forgotten all about their fool plan concernin'

Auntie Lou. What Grandpa said now made me realize that they still meant business. I twisted around so that I could hear better.

"Are you a-feelin' up to havin' some company, Lou? Been awhile since we had anyone in."

Now Grandpa knew that Lou had no objection to company. She could whip up a meal jest as tasty as any cook in the county. It was Grandpa and Uncle Charlie who usually went thumbs-down on the company idea.

Lou looked at Grandpa with interest showin' in her face— she didn't suspect a thing.

"Sure," she said. "Sounds fun! Did you have anyone particular in mind?"

Boy, does he! I could have said, but didn't. I listened hard, curious to find out who had finally passed Grandpa's and Uncle Charlie's tests.

"Well, thought maybe we could sorta start with the Rawleighs. Seem like nice folk. Kinda like to get to know them better."

Lou's blue eyes opened wide but she said nothing. I could almost see her thoughts twirlin' round.

It just so happened that Mrs. Rawleigh was a widow lady, a rather attractive one, too, as middle-aged ladies go. She only had one child, a son in his twenties. They owned a neat and prosperous farm to the east of us. Mrs. Rawleigh had used hired help on the farm for many years, but in the last few years Jedd was doing the farmin' on his own.

I thought that I could tell what Lou was thinkin', and it was on the widow—not the son—that her thoughts were centered. She tried to keep her voice very even, but I caught the tremble of excitement in it.

"Sure, that's fine—good idea. Did you have any special time in mind?"

Grandpa was feeling pleased with himself. His plan was working well.

"Kinda wondered if next Sunday dinner would be all right."

"That'll be fine. Sure, jest fine."

I felt the fear and anger risin' up in me and then I looked at Lou. She was stealin' little sideways glances at Grandpa. There was a question in her eyes, but humor, too, and I knew that she was thinkin', *You old fox you—and you never let on!*

And suddenly I wanted to snicker. This could turn out to be downright fun if I could jest keep Jedd from takin' Grandpa's bait; and that wasn't going to be an easy task with the bait as pretty as it was.

I was glad that I had been watchin' Auntie Lou. Knowin' what I did I would never have taken the turn of thought that Auntie Lou did. It wouldn't hurt none if I kinda helped those thoughts of hers to do a bit of growin' before Sunday arrived.

All week Auntie Lou worked on the house and the meal. She must've changed her mind about what she'd be servin' at least four times. She even tried new desserts out on us. They were all good, and I was quite willing to be one of her guinea pigs.

At every opportunity I tried to drop subtle hints or ask leading questions. She didn't always follow my sneaky thinkin' and jest looked at me searchingly. Still I kept workin' away at it.

"Do you think Grandpa is lookin' happier these days? Seems he's kinda different somehow"—to which Lou replied that it was prob'ly due to anticipation about Great-grandpa's comin' to join us. After several other seemingly unsuccessful tries, I decided that I was going to have to be a bit more obvious.

"How long has Mrs. Rawleigh been a widder?" I was licking cake batter from a mixing bowl.

"Oh, about eleven years now, I guess—maybe more."

"Sure seems funny."

"Seems funny that someone's a widow?"

"No. Seems funny that no one's noticed how purty she is and married her long before now."

"I hear tell one or two have tried, but she wasn't of that mind."

"Really? Who?"

"Oh—Orvis Bixley."

"Orvis Bixley? No wonder she wasn't interested."

"Nothing so wrong with Orvis Bixley."

"He's old."

"To you maybe, but he's not so awful much older than the widow Rawleigh."

"He seems it. She still looks young—and purty, too."

"You said that."

"Oh, yeah." I licked without talkin' for a while, then set aside the bowl.

"Who else?" I inquired.

"Who else what?"

"Who else tried to marry the widow Rawleigh?"

She looked at me with that questioning look of hers as if to sort out jest what I was fishin' for. I avoided her eyes.

"I don't know," she finally said. "Some hired man that she had at one time, I guess. I don't know his name."

I didn't know jest how to make my point and tie up this conversation.

"Sure wouldn't blame *any* man for takin' a likin' to her." I put lots of stress on the *any*. I left. I could feel Lou's eyes on my departin' back.

Lou took a break later in the day to sit in the shade on the back porch and do some fancy stitchin' on a pillowcase. I knew that I still had some unfinished business, but I hoped that I had given her somethin' to think on earlier. I came right to the point.

"Do you think that Grandpa would be happier married again?"

She looked up quickly.

"I don't know."

"Wonder why he never did?"

"He was too busy carin' for us I s'pose."

That was exactly what I had wanted her to say.

"Do you think we've been selfish?"

"Selfish? How?"

"Well, if it weren't for us, he could be married again and happy." I tried to make it sound like there was no way that Grandpa could have any measure of happiness while unmarried.

"There's still plenty of time," Lou said absentmindedly. "Pa is still young enough to have lots of years of happiness with another wife—if he so chooses."

"And we won't stand in his way anymore?"

"I don't know that we ever—"

"I jest mean that we're old enough now—me and you— that iffen Grandpa wanted to marry again, we could sorta look after ourselves."

"What are you driving at?" Lou eyed me suspiciously.

"Well," I said, and my words were honest, even if my meaning wasn't. "I somehow got the feelin' last Sunday when Grandpa asked about havin' the Rawleighs to dinner that there was more to it than he was lettin' on."

Now that was a mouthful. Lou took it the way I had hoped she would. Slowly she reached out to me with a quiet little smile.

"You rascal," she said. "You don't miss a thing, do you? Well, I'm glad that you're not upset. Maybe nothing will come of it anyway." She thought for a bit.

"Okay, so Pa wants to get to know the widow Rawleigh better. I don't know her well, but if Pa likes her, she has my full approval. She seems nice enough. If Pa, and I say *if* he likes her, then I, *and* you, we won't say anything. We'll jest do our best to make everything as pleasant for Pa as we can. I'm kinda glad that you caught on to it, too. Now I know that I can count on you to help me.

"Now above all, we mustn't seem to push or fuss. That would jest make them self-conscious and uncomfortable. They have to work this out for themselves in their own way—and time. And we disappear—if we can.

"Remember, until Pa wishes to state his own case, we play ignorance. Okay?"

"Okay," I agreed.

"There's only one little thing that bothers me."

"What's that?"

"That Jedd! To think that I might end up with him for a brother!" Lou made a sour face and shuddered. "But that's our secret, okay?"

I grinned. It was sure okay with me all right.

"Not so fond of Jedd myself," I said.

"Well, let's try not to let it show if we can help it."

I nodded, feelin' sorta like takin' on something big. Lou didn't care much for Jedd. That sure helped my situation a heap!

I was jest about to draw a deep breath in relief when a funny thought went flittin' through my brain; and with it came a feelin' of uneasiness. *What if Grandpa really did go and fall for the widow Rawleigh?* I reckoned that I'd hate to lose Grandpa jest about as much as I'd hate to lose my Auntie Lou. Naw! Grandpa'd have more sense than to go and do a thing like that. Still it would bear some watchin'. Anyway, I could only handle one worry at a time, so I'd have to let that one pass for the time bein'.

I picked up the milk pails and puckered my lips into a whistle, trying to drum up confidence that I wasn't too sure I felt. Anyway, the whistlin' helped some.

Chapter 6

Sunday Dinner

Saturday was cloudy with a stiff wind blowin'. I saw Grandpa look out the window to check the skies several times. He seemed really worried that his well-laid plans might all come to ruin. A few times I saw him and Uncle Charlie sort of huddled together talkin' in low tones. I pretended not to notice, although I was near dyin' to know what was being said.

Lou was busy with final preparations in the house. She even toyed with the idea of opening up the front parlor, but Grandpa said that it wasn't necessary. The parlor had been closed and all of the furniture covered with sheets ever since Grandma had died. When I was little I was scared of that room; then one day Auntie Lou took me by the hand and showed me under all the sheets—nothing but furniture. There was some pretty fine furniture too—even an organ.

At first Grandpa had said, "Men don't have time to spit and polish all that fancy stuff." Later he changed it to, "No use Lou havin' to fuss with that; she's already got enough to do." But I think that the real reason for the parlor staying closed had something to do with Grandma and how Grandpa missed her. Anyway, in spite of Lou's offer, the parlor again stayed closed. The dinner table was laid as usual in our big kitchen with the family living quarters off to one side. Grandpa said that Lou kept it pretty enough for *any* company.

After the scare that the weather gave us on Saturday, Grandpa was relieved to see the clouds blown away and the sun comin' out again on Sunday mornin'.

I hadn't seen him in such good spirits for a long time, and Auntie Lou and I exchanged a wink as we watched him polishin' his shoes and brushin' his hat. Lou was convinced that he had taken a shine to the widow all right; and I might even have begun to worry myself if I hadn't overheard Grandpa whisper to Uncle Charlie, "Remember, this is jest for a get-acquainted like—no pushin' today." Uncle Charlie nodded and grinned.

The ride to church was pleasant. Even the service was okay. The singin' was really good—jest as though the folks were like birds glad to see the sun again and wanting to sing their hearts out. Old Parson White brought a sermon that even boys could understand and didn't mind listenin' to. Even Willie Corbin left off carvin' initials in the pew and paid attention; Jack Berry only pulled out his warty frog to shove it toward the girls once. I was sure that after church he'd be mad at himself for missin' so many good chances.

While folks stood around out in the sunshine after the service, Grandpa removed his hat and approached the widow Rawleigh to check that their plans to come to dinner were all in order. I saw some eyebrows go up. Mrs. T. Smith and Mrs. P. Smith were talkin' nearby. Mrs. T. stopped mid-sentence and gave the old-eyebrow trick to Mrs. P. She responded. I knew that they were thinkin' the same way as Auntie Lou was concernin' this Sunday dinner date. I snickered and ducked behind some of the boys so folks wouldn't wonder if I was up to some kind of mischief.

Grandpa, in his innocence, went right on chattin' with widow Rawleigh, and she turned coy and kinda flirty right there before all those people. Grandpa still didn't seem to notice—but others sure did. Grandpa took his leave with a lift of his hat, and Mrs. Rawleigh sorta giggled and lifted her chin.

She deliberately looked around at the other ladies present to see just what kind of an impression this had made on all of them. She wasn't disappointed.

I headed for my spot at the back of the wagon and got set to remove my shoes jest as soon as the church was out of sight.

I knew that Auntie Lou was in a real hurry to get home so that she could finish the dinner preparations. The table was already laid and a fine bunch of mixed flowers stood on the small table by the window. The meal had been left in big simmerin' pots on the fire-banked kitchen stove. Things would be nigh about ready to tie into when we got home. Grandpa pushed the team a bit. He was in a hurry, too.

The wagon had hardly stopped rollin' when Auntie Lou's feet hit the ground and she was off to the kitchen almost on the run. Grandpa sort of misread her eagerness, and I saw him give Uncle Charlie an elbow and nod toward Auntie Lou. They grinned like two schoolboys who had jest put a garter snake in the teacher's desk.

We didn't have to wait too long for the Rawleighs. I guess they were kinda excited about the whole thing, too. By the time they arrived Auntie Lou had everything in order. She appeared as cool as though she had spent the day swayin' in a hammock in the shade instead of rushin' around a kitchen over a hot stove.

Grandpa made short work of the preliminaries. He was about to seat the folks at the table when Lou stepped over and did it with such grace that no one could question her right to do so. She placed Grandpa at his usual place at the far end of the table with Mrs. Rawleigh to his right. Beside Mrs. Rawleigh sat Uncle Charlie. Jedd was seated at Grandpa's left and beside Jedd, me. Lou took the hostess' chair opposite Grandpa.

We all bowed our heads while Grandpa said grace. As well as bein' thankful for the food, he thanked the Lord for "kind friends to share our table and our fellowship." I'm sure that the widow Rawleigh thought that was awfully cute of Grandpa, for she slipped him the most meaningful little smile when he raised his head.

The meal went well enough. The grown folks did most of

the talkin'. Occasionally Jedd made a comment. It was usually a little off-beat, it seemed to me, and I got the impression
that in spite of his prospect of becomin' a rich farmer, the guy
really wasn't too bright. The widow Rawleigh didn't see it that
way, and no matter what Jedd said she beamed her smile of
approval. The whole thing sorta rubbed against me. There
was no way that I wanted this guy for an uncle—no matter
which way it might come about.

After the dinner and all the comments about how fine the
food was, Lou suggested that everyone have their second cup
of coffee on the back porch. That way we could all get out of
the over-warm kitchen. Folks agreed and soon everyone was
seated on the porch sippin' coffee—except Uncle Charlie. He
gulped his.

A bit of a breeze rustled through the leaves of the honeysuckle vine. It played with Lou's hair, too—whispin' it in little
curls around her flushed pink cheeks. As I looked at her I
thought that her eyes seemed even bluer—maybe because of
the blue dress that she was wearin'. I held my breath, hopin'
that Jedd wouldn't take a good look at her. A fellow would
have to have corn cobs in his brain not to see jest how pretty
Auntie Lou was. I was about to blurp something out to Jedd to
try to keep his attenton when Auntie Lou herself saved the
day.

"If you'll all jest excuse me," she said, "I think I'll put the
food away."

The widow knew perfectly well that a woman couldn't
properly put away another woman's leftovers, so she gave a
sweet smile and remarked, "When you're ready to wash up,
dear, just call."

Lou only smiled, then was gone. I followed her in. She
glanced back at the porch.

"Josh," she said, "I know that it's a heap to ask, but do
you s'pose you could find some way to entertain Jedd?"

I thought hard and was lucky enough to recall that I'd
heard that Jedd Rawleigh liked fishin'.

"Hear he likes fishin'," I said. "I could take him to the
crik."

"On Sunday?"

"Not to fish," I hurried on, "jest to look. If he likes fishin',
then he must like the water, too."

This earned me a big smile and a quick hug.

"Good idea," Lou whispered.

Only for Auntie Lou would I agree to take someone down to
my part of the crik—especially someone like Jedd Rawleigh. I
was about to drag myself back out to the porch to do the invit-
in' when I got a bright idea. I'd take him to the part of the crik
the farthest away from the house. The trail wasn't too well
worn goin' that way, but I was sure that I could still follow it. I
never went over that way much because the crik flowed wide
and shallow there and there were no holes for fishin'. The
banks were covered with marsh grass and scrub willow, and
the whole area was spongy and more like swampland than
anything else.

My eyes must have reflected what I was thinkin', for Auntie Lou looked at me rather closely.

"You don't mind?"

"Naw, I don't mind." I tried to sound very off-hand about
it.

I slipped to the porch now with almost a bounce to my
step. Grandpa was listenin' to the widder tell about her problems with hired men and how relieved she was to have dependable Jedd now doing the farmin'.

I poked Jedd. "Care to take a little walk?"

He clambered up and grinned at me, and we started off.
We rounded the house and I stopped at the front porch as
though I'd had a last-minute thought and pulled off my shoes
and socks.

"Never did feel comfortable in Sunday shoes," I said, and I
carefully rolled up the legs of my Sunday pants.

Jedd jest smiled, quite willing to accept my boyish whim.
Truth was, there was no way that I wanted to be wearin' my
Sunday shoes where I was intendin' to go.

"Hear ya like fishin'."

He grinned again, then quickly sobered.

"Ma won't let me fish on Sunday."

"Oh, I don't fish Sunday either; jest thought that ya might like to check out the crik for some future day."

"Sure." He was grinnin' again.

We started out toward the back cow pasture. I glanced around to check if we were being noticed. The widow Rawleigh, Grandpa, and Uncle Charlie still sat on the porch. From my own experience, added to what I was able to piece together from talking to Auntie Lou—plus usin' my imagination jest a bit—I figure that the rest of that Sunday afternoon went something like this: Uncle Charlie wasn't doin' so great at carryin' his part of the conversation, and when Lou gave him a nod from the kitchen door, he gladly hurried over to her.

"I know that Mrs. Rawleigh said for me to call her for the washing-up, but she and Pa seem to be havin' such a nice visit. Do you mind dryin', Uncle Charlie?"

Lou said it with her cutest I-know-what's-really-goin'-on smile and Uncle Charlie jest grinned and got a towel. Truth was, he much preferred being in the kitchen with Lou to sittin' miserably listenin' to that chitchat on the porch.

The dishes were done in jig time, and Uncle Charlie reluctantly eased himself toward the door again. You see with the front parlor closed off, the only way out of the house was the back door, so for Uncle Charlie it was either stay cooped up inside or else pass by the two guardin' his exit. He hesitated a moment, then stepped out onto the porch.

"Oh, my," said the widow, suddenly come to remembrance seein' Uncle Charlie materialize before her. "How the time has been flyin'! I'm sure that dear Louisa must be ready with those dishes by now."

"All done," said Uncle Charlie, and Grandpa favored him with a hard look. Uncle Charlie chose to ignore it. "Jest finished."

Uncle Charlie appeared to be going right on down the steps so Grandpa stopped him.

"Where did the young'uns git to?"

"Went fer a walk, I take it."

"That's nice," smiled Grandpa, picturin' Jedd and Lou strollin' through knee-deep meadows hand and hand, she wearin' a flower that he'd pinned in her hair.

Wasn't quite that way though. Jedd and I were sloggin' through marshy ground fightin' willow bushes. I was all right. I was barefoot and I made good and sure that my pant legs stayed rolled up to above my knees. Jedd wasn't farin' as well. His Sunday shoes were smeared with mud, and even though he lifted his pant legs some in the soggier spots, they were still splashed and spotted. He puffed as he pushed his way through the heavy growth. I kept assurin' him every few minutes that it wouldn't be long now, and we'd be there any minute, and the crik was jest beyond thet next clump.

As for Auntie Lou, she had confided to Uncle Charlie that she thought she would take a little walk. Supposin' that she had prearranged to meet "someone," he jest smiled and said, "Good idea." So after the dishes were done, Auntie Lou picked up a book and prepared to make her escape. She was more resourceful than Uncle Charlie. She climbed quietly and carefully through the kitchen window and walked down to the pond where she sat and read until she was needed to serve afternoon refreshments.

Uncle Charlie remained only a few moments on the back porch and then moved on, mumblin' something about stretchin' his legs a bit and checkin' the horses. That left Grandpa and the widow. Guess the day dragged somewhat for him. He never was much of a talker, but he wasn't a bad listener and the widow seemed to prefer it that way.

When the sun swung around to the west, Auntie Lou decided that she'd best get back to the kitchen and get the tea on. She entered the kitchen the same way that she had left, gently coaxin' her full skirts over the window ledge.

I finally did stumble upon the crik—such as it was up that way. Sure weren't much to brag about as criks go and even the slow Jedd recognized that it wasn't housing any fish. I seemed right surprised and disappointed about it all, though I did manage to keep from tellin' an outright lie. We started back, sloshin' our way through marsh and muck. Jedd's Sunday-go-meetin' clothes looked worse all the time, and I began to wonder if I'd gone a mite too far.

When we got back to the house, we were later than we should have been. Tea and strawberry shortcake were all laid out. Uncle Charlie had again put in an appearance. The widow hadn't slowed down much, though she was concerned about the lateness of her Jedd.

When she got her first good look at him, her eyebrows shot up so high that they nearly disappeared into her pompadour hair style.

Me, I looked fine. I had carefully rolled down my pant legs, easin' out the creases the best that I could, and brushed off the loose twigs and bits of dirt. I'd also cleaned my feet off with water from the rain barrel, dried them on the grass and put my socks and shoes back on. I was most as good as new. Jedd, now, was a different matter. His shoes and socks were a sight, and his pant legs didn't look so great either. He had twigs and spider webs and other clutter still clingin' to his clothes and his hair.

When the widow finally caught her breath, she gasped, "Where have you been?"

I let Jedd answer. He gave a rather weak smile. "To the crik."

Now I saw Grandpa's eyebrows go up. He knew all of the paths to the crik and every inch of the territory through which the crik flowed. I knew that it was obvious to him jest what part of the crik we had visited. He looked at Jedd, then at me, Jedd's clothes, my clothes. He frowned. Something here was strange and would bear his checkin' out later after the company left.

Mrs. Rawleigh went to work on Jedd. I thought that he looked rather like a big overgrown schoolboy as she brushed and wiped and scolded. Eventually she declared him fit to partake of the strawberry shortcake, though he still didn't look none too good.

As soon as we were finished at the table, Uncle Charlie went with Jedd to get the team, and the widow turned her attention back to Grandpa.

"This has been just delightful, Daniel."

She stretched as many syllables out of his name as her tongue could possibly manage.

"We must do it again soon."

Grandpa looked uncomfortable. I could see tiny beads of sweat standin' on his forehead, but he remained a true gentleman and a perfect host.

"Very nice," he smiled. "It's been our pleasure. Very nice."

He seemed to get a sudden inspiration.

" 'Course it's gettin' mighty close to harvest time now. 'Fraid I'm gonna have to forsake pleasure fer a while and pursue work instead."

Mrs. Rawleigh beamed. So clever this man, and such a gentleman.

"Of course, but one must rest on the Lord's Day, even in harvest. We'll expect you to return our good pleasure and join us for Sunday dinner one day soon."

"That would be most gracious of you and we'd be delighted to do so."

Grandpa was really squirmin' now. It was quite obvious, even to him, that the widow had somehow gotten entirely the wrong idea.

"Next Sunday then?"

"Next Sunday." Grandpa forced a weak smile.

The widow turned to the rest of us and nodded her goodbye.

"And again thank you for the lovely dinner, dear," she said to Auntie Lou. "You are indeed a real credit to your father." She turned those admiring eyes full on Grandpa and flashed him a most inviting smile. Grandpa's hand went up to ease his collar. I'm sure that he felt he would choke.

Eventually we got them headin' for home. Grandpa walked back to the house sheddin' his tight collar and shakin' his head. Things had somehow gone all wrong, it seemed. He decided to hold his judgment until he got Lou's report on the day. Surely she had gotten to know Jedd sometime during the long hours. Grandpa sat down at the kitchen table and mopped his brow.

"Nice folks." He was speakin' to Lou. Uncle Charlie and I both knew that, even if we were sittin' there.

"Um humm."

"Had a nice visit with Mrs. Rawleigh."

"We saw that," said Lou with a twinkle and Grandpa's face reddened. He tried to ignore it and went on.

"Did you get a chance to visit with Jedd?"

"Much as I cared to," she promptly responded.

"When?"

"At the table."

Now Grandpa knew full well how much visitin' Lou and Jedd had done at the table. I doubt that there was even so much as "Pass the butter." He gazed up at Lou. She looked back evenly, then rose and crossed over to behind his chair, and in her little girl way put her arms round his neck.

"Oh, Pa," she said as she laid her cheek against his. "It needn't spoil anything—honest. I just can't stand Jedd Rawleigh, that's all. But if you—if you enjoy the company of Mrs. Rawleigh, that's fine. I promise. I won't interfere; I'll be as agreeable and as—as—"

He jerked upright and looked at Lou like she'd lost her senses. Grandpa was gettin' the full message now.

"You think that I—that I—you think that I care in some way fer the widow?"

"Don't you?"

Grandpa's face was beet red and the cords in his neck showed up plain.

" 'Course not!" he stormed. " 'Course not."

"Then why—"

"I jest wanted you to—" Grandpa was trapped and he knew it. He couldn't let Lou know that he was out to get her married off; he couldn't lie either. He finally sputtered to a close.

"Jest—jest forgit it. Forgit it all. It was all kinda a mistake—"

"But the widow Rawleigh," cut in Auntie Lou.

"What about her?" Grandpa almost snapped, and he never snapped at Lou.

"We're invited there for Sunday dinner."

"We'll go as we said." Grandpa was definite on that.

"But she thinks—" Lou hesitated.

"Thinks what?"

"Well," said Lou rather perplexed by the whole new situation, "bein' a woman myself and seein', I'm sure she thinks that you *do* care."

"What in the world would ever give her that idea?" Grandpa huffed.

"Well, you extended the invitation, you talked—alone—for many hours."

Grandpa swung around.

"Where were the rest of you anyway? Charlie! Where did you disappear to so convenient? You could've listened to the account of her goiter operation jest as easily as me. Where'd you get to anyway? And Boy—" but I was already up the steps on the way to change my clothes and get to the woodpile. Thought that it wouldn't hurt to chop a bit of extra wood; Lou must have used an awful lot in that old kitchen stove in order to cook a meal like that.

The topic of the Rawleighs was not discussed again. We did go there for Sunday dinner as promised, but we didn't stay late, and Grandpa had given us all strict orders before we left home that no one was to desert the room. We thanked our host and hostess after a rather uneventful stay and headed for home.

Mrs. Rawleigh wasn't half the cook that Auntie Lou was. Grandpa, more with silence than words, ordered the whole case dismissed.

Mentally I crossed Jedd Rawleigh from my list—a bit smugly, I'm afraid.

Chapter 7

Hiram

The whole episode did manage to shake Grandpa up some, and I thought that maybe he'd drop any further efforts—but no such luck. I had gone to bed and was almost asleep when I heard the coffeepot rattlin' and the murmurin' of voices from the kitchen. I hiked myself out from under the warm covers and eased my way down the stairs. Sure enough, the two of them were at it again.

". . . weren't either my own fault," Grandpa was sayin'. "I was deserted, that's all."

"Well, the first mistake came by pickin' on a widder. We shoulda thought how it'd look. Tongues are still waggin'."

Grandpa took a swallow of coffee that was too hot. I could hear him gulping in air to cool his tongue.

"Whole thing was ridiculous. How people could think that I'd be—I'd be—." He couldn't find words to express his feelin', so he jest ended with a "humph."

There was the sound of Uncle Charlie pursin' his lips and suckin' in air and then a long contented sigh after the hot coffee washed down his throat. His chair hit the floor to rest on all four legs again.

"So we struck out," he said matter-of-factly. "Nobody said that we were gonna git on base first time at bat. We 'xpected that it would take some time and some doin', so we don't quit now. We keep on a-lookin' before some young punk decides to do some lookin' on his own.

"You see those faces at church? Ya saw what happened last week? That there young Anthony Curtis, without a nickel to his name or a roof to put over his head, walked right up to Lou, twistin' his hat in his hands 'til he nearly wore out the brim. He asked her outright iffen he could call."

"I didn't know 'bout that," Grandpa replied with concern in his voice.

"We were lucky this time. The guy's got a face like a moose. But someday—someday it'll be a good-looker and Lou will forgit to look past the face."

"Did you hear Lou's answer?"

" 'Course I did. She said she was awful sorry-like, but she was awful busy gettin' ready fer the arrival of her grandpa from the east, and after that it would be harvest and all."

"Good for Lou." Grandpa chuckled with relief. "She can set 'em down iffen she wants to."

"That weren't the *real* reason though."

" 'Course not. Like you say, the guy ain't exactly a good-looker."

"That weren't the reason either."

"No?"

"No." Charlie paused. "It was Nellie Halliday. Lou knows that Nellie has had a crush on that there Anthony Curtis ever since she was twelve years old. Lou didn't want to hurt her."

"Nellie Halliday?" Grandpa chuckled again. "That's sorta like a moose and a porcupine."

Uncle Charlie was in no mood to appreciate Grandpa's humor. "This ain't gettin' us nowhere. Let's get down to business."

"Who should we try for next?"

"You chose Jedd Rawleigh," said Uncle Charlie; "how 'bout me havin' a crack at it now?"

"Fair enough—long as you stick to the list we made up."

"I'll stick to the list."

Uncle Charlie pored over the list, mentally examining each candidate. Grandpa waited.

"Hiram—Hiram Woxley. He looks the most likely man to me of who we've got here. Boy, there seems to be a dry spell of first-rate men 'round here."

"Never noticed it before we started lookin' fer a proper fella fer Lou. Thought the place was crawlin' with 'em. Everywhere I go I—"

I left. I'd heard enough.

Hiram Woxley was a bachelor. No worry about a widowed mother there. For all I knew Hiram could have hatched under the sand. He had moved into the area fully grown and already on his own. Never had heard anything about any kin.

He was a decent enough fellow—about thirty, always clean-shaven and neat, quiet yet kinda forceful, attended church regularly, and stayed out of the way of girls and kids. He had a big well-kept farm to the south of town; I was sure that the farm, more than the man, had to do with his bein' on the list.

I laid in bed a long time thinkin' about Hiram Woxley. What had I heard about him? Most things ever said about him were good. In fact, I couldn't right remember any disagreeable thing that I could put my finger on.

I was gettin' sleepier and sleepier and my mind jest refused to keep workin' on it when it suddenly hit me—his money! Word had it that Hiram Woxley was tight-fisted. In fact, I'd been in the hardware store one time when Hiram was making some purchases. He tried to argue—quietly but stubbornly— the price of everything that he bought. Heard the clerk say after he'd left that he always hated to see him come through the door. Rumor had it that he would about as soon lose a finger as part with a dollar. Surely I ought to be able to use that to some advantage. I made up my mind before givin' in to sleep that come Sunday I'd see if I could find some way to sorta chat a bit with Hiram Woxley—that is, if I could get near him. As I said, he wasn't much for kids.

On Sunday mornin' I managed to somehow talk Auntie Lou into wearin' her fanciest dress. It was the one that Grandpa had sorta insisted that Lou buy for Mary Smith's weddin' last spring. Grandpa liked to have Lou look her best, and even though she bucked at the price, he finally talked her into it. Auntie Lou did look like a million in that outfit.

When she came down the stairs to leave for church, I saw Grandpa and Uncle Charlie exchange worried looks. I could see that they were afraid with Lou walkin' around lookin' like that, some young fella was bound to get ideas before they had a chance to steer things in the right direction.

Lou went on out and I followed her, but I heard Grandpa whisper to Uncle Charlie, "Maybe it'll be all right. Hiram has eyes, too."

Uncle Charlie nodded. We left for church.

After the service I headed for the yard to see if I could spot old Hiram. The place was buzzin'. Everyone's mind was on the fact that the old Parson White had informed the church board of his wishes to retire before too long and that they should commence the search for a new man. Every tongue was waggin'. Most people were sure that they could never properly replace the well-loved parson. Sounded as though they would have been content to work him right into his grave. Questions were flyin' back and forth—not that they expected anyone to have any worthwhile answers. Could they ever find anyone who would fit in as well as Parson and Mrs. White had done, and should they look for a man who gave inspiring addresses or one who understood and cared for the people? They all seemed to assume that you couldn't have both wrapped in the self-same package.

I shrugged my way through it all. It meant nothin' to me. Some of the older boys were beginnin' to question this whole idea of church and why any red-blooded, adventure-seekin' boy needed it anyway. It was more for old folks and kids. I thought about it sometimes, too. Anyway, it sure didn't bother me none who the old man was who stood up at the front in the black suit and read from the Book. Guess one could do it 'bout as well as another.

I found Hiram over near the fence with some of the other single fellows. It wasn't hard to figure out the game that was goin' on. It was "ogle-the-girls," or whatever you want to call it. As each of the girls made an appearance she was rated. The fellows gave their ratings with grins, elbows, nudges, and comments. Everyone there seemed to understand jest how the system worked.

I stood there quietly, knowin' that they'd feel me too young to join in if they should notice me. Their full attention was on the church entrance as they waited for another candidate to make her appearance. In the meantime I inched my way cautiously a little closer to Hiram Woxley.

One by one the girls appeared and were judged by the fellows. Finally I saw Auntie Lou's head appear above the crowd on the steps. By almost a miracle it seemed that the whole crowd cleared around her as she stopped to chat with the parson's wife.

The sun was shining right down on her, reflectin' a shimmer of light on the curls that fell to her shoulders. Her eyes were shining and even from where we stood you could see the blue of them. She was smiling—a beautiful, typically Auntie Lou smile, full of warmth and pleasure in living. Her dress was beautiful, but as I looked at her, even I could see that she would have been pretty even if she'd been wearin' a feed sack.

Every guy around me seemed to hold his breath, and then as she moved on they all let it out at once. "Toad" Hopkins threw his hat in the air and let out a whoop. Shad Davies bellowed, "Whoo-ee!" while Burt Thomas and Barkley Shaw started to punch each other in the ribs, grinning like they were plumb crazy. Things finally settled down some.

"Wow," said Joey Smith, "some looker!"

I figured that it was time to make my presence known. I took a big gulp of air.

"Well, she oughta be." I tried hard to sound real disgusted. "Coulda bought me all the fishin' gear I've a hankerin' for and a .22 rifle, too, for the money that her outfit cost my Grandpa."

I didn't hang around to see what effect my words had, but pushed my way through the knot of fellows as though the thought of it all still made me mad. I figured I had at least given old Hiram something to be a-thinkin' on. Maybe it would work, maybe it wouldn't; I didn't know, but I'd keep workin' on it. Bit by bit a fella should be able to get the message across that a wife could end up costin' a man a powerful lot of money. I was bankin' on the fact that Hiram Woxley would want to be good and sure that she was worth it.

Chapter 8

Surprises

Uncle Charlie had fulfilled his duty in gettin' the invitation to Hiram Woxley all right, but he was not able to make it for the next Sunday's dinner. It seemed that there were others in the area who saw Hiram as a good prospect for their daughters. He had agreed to grace our humble home with his presence in two Sundays. I was glad for the breathin' time.

I said nothin' at all to Lou about the stir that she caused when she left the church—saw no reason to. Lou wasn't the kind that would let it go to her head, but still I felt that it would serve no good purpose for her to be a knowin'.

Grandpa had been keepin' a sharp eye on the south field, and on Tuesday he decided that it was ready to put the binder to it.

I loved harvest time, even if I knew it meant school again soon. Our school always started a little late to give the farm boys a chance to help their pas. When we did get back to class, the teacher worked us like crazy to get us caught up to where we should be. We really didn't mind the extra work. We were glad for a chance to have the late summer and early fall days.

With Grandpa and Uncle Charlie now in the fields all of the chores fell to me. That was all right, though I was pretty tired some nights. A few times I could hardly wait for Grandpa to call, "Bedtime, Boy," but I always managed to hang on.

I felt that with Hiram Woxley expected in a week-and-a-half, Uncle Charlie and Grandpa had no other immediate plans for Auntie Lou, so I kinda relaxed and let my thoughts go to other things.

I figured that it was about time for the fish in the crik to really start bitin'. I was anxious for a chance to get a try at them. I kept my eyes open for a break in my work that would give me a little fishin' time.

Lou was busy, too. There was stuff from the garden that needed preservin', and hungry men to feed every day and lunches to fix for me to run to the field, plus all of her usual household chores. She didn't seem to mind it, though, but like me, she was good and ready for bed come nightfall.

Lou was working on a batch of bread and I was splittin' up some wood to get a little ahead so I could work in that fishin' trip when I heard a wagon comin'. I recognized Mr. T. Smith's team even before it turned into our lane. It was kind of unusual for a neighbor to come calling during harvest, so my head came up rather quick-like. Mr. T. pulled his horses up and flipped the reins. I went forward to say a howdy, more out of curiosity than friendliness. It was then that I spied an elderly man beside him on the high wagon seat.

He was dressed in a brown tweedy suit rather than in work clothes. His hat was a jaunty small-brimmed affair—not wide-brimmed to shed rain and sun like the locals wore. He had a clean-shaven face except for a carefully trimmed white mustache. I sized him up pretty good in the brief time I had, then looked again to study his face. In his eyes I saw a twinkle that made me take to him right away, but I held myself back. I wished that Mr. T. would speak up and explain the presence of the stranger before I showed rudeness by asking.

"Howdy," I said, including them both. That much I felt sure was safe without bein' rude—Grandpa wouldn't tolerate "lip" from a youngster.

"Howdy," Mr. T. replied, but the older gent just gave me an amused smile. "Brought yer great-granddaddy."

My eyes jerked back to the old man, and at the same time my blood started churnin' all through me. This was him? Sure wasn't the package that I'd been expectin'. There were no baggy unkempt pants, no tobacco-stained chin, no glassed-over watery eyes. This alert, well-kept gentleman with the sparkle in his eyes was my great-grandpa?

Blood went pounding through my head, and I jest couldn't seem to think or move. I had me a lot of feelings that I couldn't put a name to—relief I guess, maybe a little leftover fear and—funny thing—jest a small amount of pride too. I suddenly realized that I was standin' there with my eyes buggin' and my mouth hangin' open.

"Howdy, Joshua." He said my name like he had said it many times before, like it was something really special to him. But the "howdy" sounded new on his tongue.

I coaxed out a rather hesitant smile and bestirred myself.

"Howdy, sir," I managed to answer.

He laughed at that—a nice, full, fun-filled laugh, and then he busied himself with gettin' down from the wagon. He took it slow and careful, but he was steady and as sure of himself as I would have been.

Mr. T. was busy setting down Great-grandpa's belongings. I reached up to give him a hand. After all was unloaded Mr. T. gathered up the reins and prepared to climb back up into the wagon.

"Wouldn't you come in, Mr. T.? Lou would be pleased to serve coffee," I asked, rememberin' some of the manners Grandpa had tried so hard to instill in me.

"No, Joshua," he answered, "I best git back to the cuttin'. Had to go in to the smithy to git some repairs done or I'd be home at it now. Seein' how I was comin' by on my way home, I was pleasured to have the company of yer great-granddaddy when I heerd he was in town and lookin' fer a way out."

"Thank you," I said. "We all most appreciate that. Grandpa will be much obliged."

"No trouble—my pleasure." He turned then to my great-grandpa. "Nice to have met you, Mr. Jones. Hope that we have the pleasure of gittin' good acquainted-like."

"And I thank you sincerely," said my great-grandpa, extendin' his hand, "for the safe and appreciated transport—and for the enjoyable company. I'm sure that we will have future opportunities to get better acquainted."

Mr. T. smiled, nodded, and turned the team in a big arc and left the yard. I came alive with excitement. I could hardly wait to show Great-grandpa to Auntie Lou—or Auntie Lou to Great-grandpa, I wasn't sure which. Something deep inside of me told me that they belonged to each other. I guess maybe it was those clear blue eyes that looked like the whole world was a fun place to be.

"Come on in, Great-grandpa." I hurried him. "I'll bring in yer things later."

He picked up one small bag, and I grabbed a couple of suitcases and we went through the gate, around to the back porch and into the kitchen.

Lou was jest lifting golden-crusted bread from the oven as we walked in. Her face was flushed and her hair curled around her forehead.

"Lou," I blurted out before she could even look up. "Great-grandpa's here."

She put down the hot pan and turned to us. For a very brief time they looked at one another, and then with a glad cry Lou rushed to him. He was ready for her, his arms held open wide. They laughed and hugged and laughed again. Anyone watchin' would never have guessed that they were seein' one another for the very first time. I saw tears on the cheeks of each of them. I wasn't sure whose tears they were. Great-grandpa squeezed Lou close.

"Louisa," he said, "little Lou. You're just like your daddy said."

"Oh, Grandpa," she pulled back now, "it's so good to have you. So good. But how did you get here?"

"A kind neighbor."

"Mr. T. Smith brought him," I offered. I wanted to be sure that they still knew that I was around.

"Sit down." Lou was still in a happy fluster. "Sit down and I'll get you some coffee. Josh, you run to the well and get some cream."

"No need for me, my dear. I drink my coffee black."

Lou nodded to Great-grandpa and turned to me again.

"Josh, do you want to whip up some grape juice for yourself?"

The grape juice was always kept on the pantry shelf. It was jest a matter of dilutin' it some with cold well water. I was even allowed the liberty of sprinklin' in a bit of sugar.

"You know," said Great-grandpa, "I think that maybe I'd prefer a bit of that grape juice, too. It was rather a warm trip sitting out there in the sun—and Lou," he added with a twinkle in his eye and a small twitch of his mustache, "just *one* slice of that delicious-smelling bread."

I fixed three glasses of the grape juice while Auntie Lou sliced some fresh bread and put out some homemade butter and crabapple jelly.

We had fun around the table. Great-grandpa told some stories about his long trip on the train—how one big lady had motion sickness, and how a little man with a funny box was discovered to have a pig in the passenger car. He also told of a mother with three small children who was havin' a very tryin' time until my great-grandpa offered to play games with the little ones. He said it made the miles go quicker for him, too. The young woman cried when she thanked him at the end of her journey.

All at once I glanced at the clock. The time had been racin' by and I had lots of chores that needed doin' before the menfolk got in from the fields. I jumped up rather suddenly and headed for the door.

"Josh," Great-grandpa called after me. I thought that he might be goin' to mention the fact that I hadn't asked to be excused, so I stood there feelin' rather sheepish.

"Josh, you are the chore-boy in harvest time I assume."

"Yes, sir."

"Do you have many chores?"

"Quite a few, sir."

He smiled.

"Let's see now." He seemed to be workin' on something as he tugged at one side of his mustache. "We should be able to come up with something better than 'sir' for you to address me by, shouldn't we?"

"Yes—Great-grandfather."

He laughed again.

"Now *that*," he said, "is really a mouthful. *That* will never do. You could drown or starve at the table before you got my attention with all of that to say."

I smiled.

"You call Daniel 'Grandpa'?"

I nodded.

"Then it can't be just grandpa or we'd never know whom you meant."

He worked on his mustache some more.

"Grandfather is *too* dignified for me." He wrinkled his nose in a humorous smile. "On the other hand, Grandpappy is not dignified enough. That leaves Gramps. What do *you* think of Gramps?"

"I rather like it, sir." I tried biting off the "sir," but it slipped out anyway. He smiled.

"Okay, Gramps it will be. Lou can call me Gramps, too, and then you'll both know whom you are talking about."

I grinned. It would be nice to share the name with Lou. I glanced again at the clock. It was gettin' late.

"Now then," said Gramps, "do you suppose an old man trailing around with you while you do the chores would slow you down too much?"

"Oh, no, sir—Gramps."

"Good! You run along and get started, and I'll get changed into the overalls that I bought in town. I'll join you as soon as I can."

I was off on a run. I knew what needed to be done and what I should tackle first to get it out of the way; I worked as quickly as I could, feeling an excitement that I couldn't put into words at the thought of Gramps comin' to join me.

Tonight my dog was a rusty brown with soft eyes and long

droopy ears. But I had little time for her after explainin' the reason for my rush.

"Ginger, ya jest gonna have to stand aside so you don't git tramped on 'cause I'm in a hurry to git as much done as I can before *Gramps* comes to help me."

The pigs must have wondered what had happened, the way that I ran with the slop-pails and chop. Then I took the grain and water to the chickens. On the lope, I left for the pasture gate to let Bossie down the lane. I didn't dare to run her and I felt all agitated at her slow walk for fear Gramps would be waitin' for me. He was, though he didn't seem at all put out about it.

His new overalls looked strange on him. He had rolled up the cuffs so that they wouldn't drag in the dirt. He wore a new pair of farmer's boots, too, and an old sweater that he referred to as his "gardenin' sweater."

We walked to the house for the milk pail, then back again to the barn. He pulled up an extra stool and watched me as the white streams of milk filled the pail with foam. As I milked he talked to me. He even talked to Bossie, and I had the strangest feelin' that at any time he might turn around and begin talkin' to Ginger, too.

We took the full pail of milk to the house, and Gramps said that sometime he'd like to give it a try—it looked easy enough. Did I think that Bossie would mind? I didn't think so. She was pretty even-tempered and never really seemed to mind anything but the pesky flies that sometimes drove her runnin' with her tail flyin' high.

By the time we were back from the house, Bossie had finished her chop. I let her out of her stanchion and we drove her down the lane and back to pasture. While we walked, Gramps told me how it had been for him growin' up as a boy in a big city back east. No open pastures or acres of trees, but all tall buildings, belchin' smoke stacks, and crowded streets. I tried to see it all in my mind, but it was pretty hard to picture, me never havin' been anywhere near a big city.

We ended my chores by carryin' wood. I was glad that I had already split it. Gramps carried his share. He could take as many sticks in a load as I could. I had to admire him.

I was about to return to the house when I remembered that Grandpa and Uncle Charlie would soon be returning with thirsty and tired teams.

"You go on in," I said to Gramps. "I think that I'll jest run on down to the barn and fork down some hay for the horses, then pump the trough full of water."

"Tell you what, you do the forking and I'll do the pumping."

He could see that I wasn't sure that I should let him.

"Go ahead. If I tire, I'll rest."

I ran for the barn and pushed the hay down through the chute into the mangers, then I measured out the chop and put each horse's portion in his chop box. I ran back to the pump-house. Gramps was still pumpin'. He didn't seem too winded and the trough was almost full. I took over and finished filling it.

Mentally I checked all the chores off the list that I kept in my mind. That was it. Everything was cared for and on time, too.

We carried in Gramps' two trunks and put them in the downstairs bedroom which had been our "guest room," though we never had overnight guests. Lou had decided that would be the best place for him—before she saw that stairs really wouldn't have slowed him down that much. The room was all repapered, fresh-painted and ready. It still seemed the most appropriate place for Gramps.

Lou had supper ready and waiting on the back of the stove. We washed ourselves and prepared to wait, but while we were still sharin' the long kitchen towel, we could hear the jingling of harness and we knew that Grandpa and Uncle Charlie would soon be there to join us.

Chapter 9

Family

Lou got the idea that it would be fun to surprise Grandpa and Uncle Charlie, them not expectin' Gramps to show up jest out of the blue like that; Gramps went along with it whole-heartedly. He looked around the kitchen to make sure that he hadn't left anything laying around that would give him away and then slipped into his new bedroom.

Grandpa and Uncle Charlie took turns at the basin, slosh-in' the warm water over their faces, necks, and arms. Then they scrubbed their hands with the strong soap and rinsed them in fresh water.

"Glad to see the mangers and the trough full, Boy," Grandpa commended me. Uncle Charlie tousled my hair but said nothin'.

They took their places at the table and Lou set on the food. Grandpa was the first to notice.

"What's the extry place?"

"Oh, my goodness," said Lou. "Can't I even count any-more?" But when she made no move to take away the plate, Grandpa became suspicious. He and Uncle Charlie were prob-ably both afraid that Lou had stolen a march on them and was doin' a little lookin' over the field on her own. She set down the last dish of food, a heaped-up bowl of new potatoes, and gave Grandpa her innocent little girl look.

"Truth is, Pa, I invited a guest for supper."

Grandpa and Uncle Charlie really looked nervous now. Uncle Charlie recovered first.

"Well—where is he?"

We weren't in the habit in our home of sittin' down to eat before the guests arrived.

"Well—he's—he's—a—in the bedroom." Lou raised her voice as she said it and Gramps took the cue, but not before Grandpa and Uncle Charlie had nearly choked on Lou's words.

Out popped Gramps in his new, but now slightly soiled, overalls and boots, his perky mustache twitchin' humorously and his blue eyes twinklin'.

"Well, I'll be," said Grandpa as though he couldn't believe his eyes. Then a general uproar followed with handshakes and manly hugs and laughter.

"How'd you git here?" Uncle Charlie finally asked. "We thought that we'd git a letter or a telly-gram telling us when to meet yer train."

"In the midst of harvest? Even a city-slicker like me knows better than to pull a stunt like that.

"I knew that once I got to town, I'd be able to either find a way out or to send word some way for you to come and get me."

We finally got back to the table where Lou's good meal was gettin' cold. The talk continued but the food didn't suffer because of it. It seemed to disappear in the usual fashion. Gramps complimented Lou over and over.

"Now that's what I've been missing since your grandmother died. Some good cooking—and," he added more thoughtfully, "someone to share it with."

We all understood his meaning.

"Well," Grandpa put in, "we all are right glad that ya decided to come on out and be with us. It's jest real good to have ya."

I was almost surprised at how heartily I was able to agree. I already loved the old man, and he had jest been in the house a few hours.

"Gramps helped with chores," I offered.

"He did?"

"Not really helped," corrected Gramps, "just sort of tagged along to chat a bit and see what goes on on a farm. Never been on one before, you know."

"But he did help," I insisted. "He carried wood and he pumped water and—"

Gramps stopped me. "Hey, Josh, you cut that out. Your Grandpa is supposed to think of me as old and worn out. You tell him stories like that and he'll put me out hoeing or such like."

Everyone laughed together.

"Fact is," continued Gramps, "I'd a lot rather hang around the kitchen and bother the cook." He winked at me and smiled. Suddenly he grew silent and thoughtful and raised his eyes heavenward.

"You'll never know how many times on my train ride out here that I thanked the Lord for my family. Must be the most awful thing in the world not to have *anybody*. I felt at first that I had no one—when Mama died—but all that I needed to do was to make connections again. Some people now, they're not that fortunate. When their partner is gone, they are alone—really alone.

"Here I am with my family—two sons, a granddaughter, and a great-grandson. My family. I am a man mightily, mightily blessed."

He smiled on us all. Lou brushed away tears unashamedly and Grandpa cleared his throat rather noisily. I swallowed hard. I had some thanks that needed sayin', too—it was that God hadn't taken seriously my prayer when I wanted to get rid of this wonderful old man. It almost made me break out into a sweat, to discover what I had been anxious to deny myself.

Gramps had talked about his "family." Sure we were a family. You didn't have to be a ma and a pa and four kids to be a family. All you needed was people livin' together and lovin' and helpin' one another. That's what made a family—blood-ties and love-bonds.

I straightened up taller in my chair. I was right proud to be a member of this family.

Chapter 10

The Fishin' Hole

I still had a hankerin' to work in some time at my fishin' hole before harvest ended and I found myself back in a stuffy schoolroom. Gradually my work was caught up and even a bit ahead so that I finally freed myself for a few hours on a Friday mornin'. It was already gittin' close to the noonday meal. If I went fishin' right away I would miss my dinner, but if I waited until after dinner it would sure cut into my fishin' time. I decided that I'd sweet talk Lou into makin' me a couple of sandwiches and givin' me an apple or two.

I was on my way to the kitchen to make my request when I noticed Gramps. He had been tired after his long journey by train, and when the excitement of meetin' us all sort of quieted down he realized jest how tired he was. The dry air bothered him a bit, too, but gradually he was pickin' up steam again. He still chored with me. He was catchin' on real good as to what needed to be done. Sometimes he would even say things like, "Now I'll take the water and feed to the chickens while you run down the lane for Bossie."

Durin' the day he read a lot or even puttered in the kitchen helpin' Lou prepare fruit or vegetables for cannin'.

Right now he was sittin' on the back porch readin' a big thick book. A sudden thought hit me. Would there be any chance—any chance at all—that Gramps would care for a trip to the crik? Even if he didn't fish, he could rest on the bank and read like Auntie Lou often did.

He grinned at me and I gathered together all of my nerve.

"I got a few extry hours here," I said. "Thinkin' of goin' down to the crik to see if the fish are bitin'. Dug up some great night crawlers in the barnyard."

At once his eyes lit up.

"Mind if I tag along?"

I relaxed then and blew the breath that I'd been holdin'.

"I'd like that."

"So would I."

He gathered up his book and hurried it back to his bedroom.

Lou was busy with some yellow beans.

"Auntie Lou," I ventured, "Gramps and me are gonna take us a little time fer fishin'. Would it be okay iffen we took a couple sandwiches?"

"Great idea," responded Auntie Lou, "then I won't have to stop in the middle of this job to fix dinner for ya."

Uncle Charlie and Grandpa were workin' with a neighborhood-cuttin'-bee, for a farmer who was laid up with a broken leg, so they wouldn't be home for dinner either.

"You run on out and bring the clothes in off the line so they won't fade in the sun; I'll git your lunch ready."

By the time I deposited the clothes on the kitchen table, Lou had our old lunch pail packed and ready to go. Gramps was ready, too, but a little concerned.

"I haven't a fish pole, Josh."

"We'll cut one."

"And no line."

"I have string in my pocket."

"A hook?"

I grinned. "Yeah, I've an extry."

We started off, me leading the way because Gramps hadn't been to the crik before.

I hadn't a moment's hesitation but headed straight for my favorite spot—the one that I had never shown anyone before. I jest hoped that today the fish were bitin'.

When the path was wide enough, we walked side by side.

"You know," admitted Gramps, "you're going to find this hard to believe, but I've never been fishing before."

I did find it hard to believe. I couldn't imagine livin' without occasional fishin'.

"You're going to have to teach me, Josh."

"I'll show ya all I know," I solemnly promised. "I jest hope they're bitin'."

We got to the crik and it looked great. The dark shadows hung on the deeper water. I could hardly wait to git started, but first I got out my jackknife and cut a pole for Gramps. Then I tied the string in the notch that I made on one end. I pulled my little bottle out of my pocket, took out a hook and attached it to the other end of the string.

"This the spot?"

"This is it." Excitement filled my voice.

"You know," said Gramps, "I rather like the looks of that small island out there in the middle. Don't you think that might be a great place to sit and fish from?"

Already Gramps showed a fisherman's instincts. I liked that. That little island was the best place along the whole crik, but you had to wade to get to it, and I wasn't sure if I should suggest that to Gramps. Now I answered promptly.

"Yep! It sure is, but ya gotta wade to git there."

"Well, let's wade."

"Ya gotta go downstream a ways where the water is shallower and cross over on the sandbar, then walk upstream and come in right there at the end—slightly to the other side. That way you won't git yer clothes all soaked."

"Lead the way," prompted Gramps. "Let's go."

I led the way. When we got to the crossin' place, I set the lunch pail on the ground alongside my pole and bent down to pull up my pant legs; I was barefoot. Gramps followed suit. Then he bent over and undid his shoes and socks. When he was finished, we picked up all of our gear and started across.

The water felt cold at first, but we gradually got used to it.

I tried to pick sandy places with few rocks 'cause I realized that Gramps hadn't been runnin' most of the summer with bare feet like I had and his feet wouldn't be tough like mine.

We got into a little deeper water as we made our way upstream, and I heard Gramps chucklin' behind me.

When I reached jest the right spot, I cut over and headed for the small island. It wasn't much more than room for two people to comfortably sit, but it did have some trees and bushes.

I heaved myself up the little bank, laid down my equipment and turned to give Gramps a hand. He handed me his pole and then clambered up the bank to join me. He was still chucklin'.

"Afraid I didn't do as good a job as you rolling up my pant legs, Josh. One slipped down mid-stream."

It sure had all right. A good two feet of overall leg was soakin' wet.

"Does Lou get riled about wet overalls?"

"Well, sorta," I answered honestly. "It's not the wet so much as the dirt that mixes with it. By the time one gits home, it's mud."

"I can see the problem," said Gramps, lookin' at the soggy leg.

"Well, then, we'll just have to dry it out, won't we?" And right there, on our little island, Gramps unclasped his overall straps and climbed out of his pants.

He picked up the wet leg and wrung all of the water out of it that he could, then he crossed to a nearby bush and spread the overalls out over the branches, with the wet leg layin' full in the sun.

"There now." His eyes twinkled as he chuckled again. "That should dry just fine by home time."

I looked at his wet underwear leg. He looked down, too.

"That won't matter any. It'll partly dry as I sit in the sun and fish; and the wet that remains will be covered with my overalls when I walk home on the dusty path, so it won't gather the dirt."

He had it all figured out.

"Let's get to fishing! Just hope that my white flannels don't scare the fish away."

He really did look a sight, trampin' around in his skinny-legged underwear, his plaid shirttails flappin' loose. I couldn't help it. I jest had to laugh and he joined right in.

I took off my denim shirt and spread it on the ground in what I considered a first-rate spot. I figured that we should protect that white underwear as much as possible or Auntie Lou might be askin' questions. Gramps settled down on the shirt and I handed him my pole. It was kinda special to me and had my favorite hook on it, but I knew that I wanted Gramps to have the best. He knew what I was doin'.

"Thank you, Joshua," he said softly.

I showed him where to drop the line and how to jiggle the pole, jest slightly, to give a bit of action to the hook under the water. I took the other pole, baited the hook, and threw it in.

We hadn't been there long when I felt a quick tug. I knew that I had one, and like every other time, I felt excitement shiver through my whole body.

Gramps got excited, too, and jumped to his feet cheerin' me on. I finally got the fish landed, and it flopped back and forth in the grass a safe distance from the water's edge. I tapped it with a rock so that it wouldn't suffer none.

"It's a dandy! It's a dandy!" Gramps kept yellin'. "You're a real fisherman, Josh, a real fisherman."

I had never seen anyone so excited about a fish before. It was a fair size, but I had caught bigger ones from this hole. Still, I was pleased with it and even more pleased at the fact that Gramps admired my accomplishment.

We kept right on fishin' even when we ate our sandwiches. Auntie Lou had really packed a terrific lunch. I thought when I looked in the pail that we could stay fishin' for the whole week without worryin' about runnin' out of food, but to the surprise of both of us, we emptied the pail of everything—sandwiches, pie, apples, and all.

We had jest finished the last of our lunch when I felt a tug on my line again. Gramps was a-whoopin' even before the fish jumped to try to free itself.

"It's a dandy! Hang on, Josh! Bring him in, Joshua! Easy now! That does it! It's a dandy! It's a dandy!"

I got that fish landed, too, and as the two laid there on the grass together, they were almost identical in size. Gramps' face was flushed with pleasure. He whipped off his hat and pounded the leg of his underwear.

"Boy, Josh," he said, "this beats a circus."

Now a circus was one thing that I'd always had a hankerin' to see, but none had ever come anywhere near our little town. I picked up on it.

"You seen a circus?"

Gramps slowed down a bit. He even put his hat back on. He settled back down on my shirt and picked up the fishin' pole. He tossed the line out carefully and began to jiggle it— jest a bit—like I had showed him.

"Yep. I've seen circuses."

"What are they like?"

As we continued fishin' Gramps described to me the trapeze acts, the jugglers, the sword swallowers, the fire eaters, and the animal acts. I sat there so amazed by it all that I sometimes even forgot to jiggle my hook.

"I know what I'd like best," I said slowly.

"What?"

"The animal acts."

"You like animals?"

"Love 'em."

"Then I guess it'a a good thing that you live on a farm."

"That's never helped me none."

"You have all kinds of animals here," responded Gramps.

"Sure, dumb ol' chickens and pigs, barn cats and cows. I don't mean that."

"I'm sure that you must have spring calves and—"

"Who would ever train a spring calf?"

"Oh," said Gramps catchin' on. "You mean animals that you can train to do special things."

"Yeah," I sorta mumbled, but I had a lot of feelin' in what I said. "Like roll over and sit up and beg and things."

Gramps jest nodded his head. He started to say something

but jest then his line jerked. Both of us were on our feet and I found myself yellin'.

"It's a dandy! Easy does it. Bring him in. That's right. Give him a little line. Bring him in again. Good work! It's a dandy!"

I don't know who was the most excited when Gramps landed that fish—him or me; but we both whooped and danced around—me in my rolled-up farm overalls, and him in his tight-legged white underwear.

When we finally stopped pattin' each other on the back, we decided that we'd better call it a day. I could tell by the sun that it would soon be chore time and besides, we could hardly wait to show Auntie Lou.

Gramps picked his overalls off the bush and tied them around his neck. He wasn't goin' to chance wet legs on the return trip. We both pulled up the legs of what we were wearin' as far as we could, then gathered our poles, the lunch pail; the fish were strung on a piece of string. We started back across the crik, me leadin' the way again.

When we reached the bank, Gramps put his overalls on again and dressed his feet. Gatherin' all of our things together, we started for home.

"We must do this again, Josh."

"I'll soon be back in school."

"Then we must try to do it at least once more before you go."

"Maybe we can—iffen I can jest keep the work caught up, maybe we can."

"I'll lend a hand," said Gramps, and I knew that he would.

Chapter 11

Number Two

All of the men of the house had been feelin' concern for Auntie Lou, though I guess none of us had expressed it to each other. Harvest and cannin' time was an awfully hard time of year for a farm woman—yet Auntie Lou was jest a slip of a girl and carryin' it all.

I tried to be sure that she always had lots of wood and water on hand without havin' to ask for it. Uncle Charlie most always picked up a dish towel when he got up from the supper table, and Grandpa stood guard at the door like a sentry to be sure that no one entered the kitchen with dirty boots or pant-leg cuffs. He needn't have botherd. We all had checked ourselves by the time we got there anyway.

Gramps was Lou's biggest help. He watched like a hawk and knew when there was a job that could use an extra pair of hands. Auntie Lou and he chatted and laughed as they worked together. They enjoyed one another, that was plain.

Gramps was the only person that I was willing to share Auntie Lou with without feelin' jealousy. I enjoyed the pleasure that they took from one another's company—but then they always included me if I was around.

In spite of the help that we all tried to give, Auntie Lou's job was still a big one; as the Sunday drew near when we were to *entertain* Hiram Woxley, I think Uncle Charlie felt a mite sorry that he had asked him, knowin' full well that it added to Lou's work.

Sunday came. Lou didn't fuss around for Hiram Woxley like she had for the widow Rawleigh—he was Uncle Charlie's guest. She would serve him a good Sunday dinner and that was that.

I still felt a bit uneasy about the whole thing. What if the fella should take a shine to Lou? Worse yet, what if she should take a likin' to him?

Anyway, there we were, right smack-dab in the middle of the Sunday that I had tried hard to pretend would never come.

We went to church as usual. I didn't pay much attention to the message that Parson White gave. It was all about "being prepared" and I wasn't plannin' on "going" for a good long time yet. I didn't like thinking about dying anyway, so I switched my mind over to something else.

I had a hard time at first findin' something that I cared to spend all that time on; then I thought of Gramps' circus and I settled back on the hard wooden bench to enjoy my stay. Of course it was the animal acts that I thought on.

I pictured myself as a ringmaster, with a tall black stove-pipe hat like Gramps had described, and a bright ruffly shirt and red swallow-tails. I didn't carry a whip—only a little pointin' stick, and I had dogs—lots of dogs, and all kinds, all sizes. They could all do different tricks, and the people roared and clapped and yelled to see us again and again. Before I had even taken my final bow, the service was over and the people were leavin' the church. I couldn't believe that time had gone so fast.

Soon we were all loaded in the wagon, headin' for home. I sat at the back. As soon as we turned the corner, I whipped off my Sunday shoes and my socks. I saw Gramps watchin' me.

"No use wearin' out good Sunday shoes 'fore ya need to," I explained.

Before I knew it Gramps had moved from his wagon seat and was easin' himself down beside me; then he, too, reached down and carefully removed his shoes. He put them far enough into the wagon so that they wouldn't jiggle out and swung his legs contentedly back and forth.

"Those rascals always have pinched me," he whispered in my ear.

When we turned in the lane, we both hurriedly put our socks and shoes back on. With Hiram comin' I supposed I would be stuck in them for the entire day.

Lou was unflurried as she finished the dinner preparations. Hiram drove in and was heartily welcomed by Grandpa and Uncle Charlie—and I guess two out of five ain't bad. It wasn't long until Lou summoned us for dinner. She placed Hiram down at the end with Grandpa and Uncle Charlie, and Gramps and I were on her right and left.

I could see that Hiram was mightily impressed with Lou's cooking and the knot started tightenin' up in my stomach again. I even refused a second piece of pie. I cast around in my mind for comments that I could make on jest how expensive it was to set such a good table, but anything that I could come up with I knew was in Grandpa's category of rudeness so I had to let them go unsaid.

As soon as the meal was over, Uncle Charlie took charge. He wasn't goin' to ball things up like Grandpa had.

"Now Lou," he said, "seein' as how you been a-workin' so hard on the cannin', bakin', an' all, you deserve ya a little rest. Why don't you jest go on out on the back porch and re-lax and visit with Hiram a bit, while yer pa and me do up these dishes."

Lou looked up, her puzzlement showin' clearly, but before she could venture a protest, Grandpa cut in quick.

"Good idee," and he almost pushed Lou toward the door. Then he went one step further. "Pa, why don't you an' Josh have ya a game of checkers. I've been tryin' to teach him, but you know that I never was the checker player that you are— an' I've forgot a lot of the good moves."

Now Grandpa was a right good checker player when he took the time to play. Fact is, he had rather made a name for himself in our community. We had played checkers a fair amount on long, quiet winter evenin's, but never before in the busy days of harvest. Even on Sundays at harvest time a man was more inclined to jest sit and relax or read, rather than to work hard on "thinkin'."

Uncle Charlie was busy banging around the dishpan and filling it with hot water from the kitchen stove's reservoir, and Grandpa was scurryin' around the table gathering up the dishes.

In preference of makin' a scene, Lou, still with a bewildered look on her face, allowed herself to be shuttled out the door and onto the back porch. Hiram grinned as he followed her, and my stomach lurched again.

"Checkers are right over there, Pa. You get them, Boy— you know where they are."

So Gramps and I were herded into the far corner of the kitchen and stationed over the red and black checkerboard.

My heart wasn't in it nor my mind on it, and I played a horrible game. I began to wonder why I wasn't losing even worse than I was; then I realized that Gramps' mind definitely wasn't on the game either.

When the noise of the clatterin' dishes was at its height, Gramps whispered to me without even liftin' his eyes from the board.

"What's going on here, Joshua?"

I was a bit surprised that he had picked it up so quickly, and for a moment I wondered jest how much I should tell him. I decided to jest blurt it all out. Boy, did I need an ally, and for some reason I had the sure feelin' that Gramps would be on my side.

"Grandpa and Uncle Charlie are lookin' to marry off Auntie Lou."

He waited a few minutes; then as Uncle Charlie rattled the cutlery, he whispered again. "Does she know it?"

"Hasn't a notion!"

I thought that I heard him say "good" but I wasn't sure.

"Is she interested?"

"Nope," I replied with confidence. I would explain more later.

This time I was sure that I heard him say "good."

"Know anything about this Hiram guy?" Gramps' eyes still hadn't left the board.

I knew that Gramps meant anything that was unfavorable.

"Only that he likes money," I whispered back, pretending hard that my next move really had me puzzled.

Gramps stood up.

"You're no match for me, Joshua," he said teasingly—"unless you work on your game. Anyway, I think that that's enough checkers for today. Let's get some air."

I saw Grandpa and Uncle Charlie look at one another nervously as Gramps and I moved toward the kitchen door. I'm sure that Gramps noticed them, too, but he never let it slow him down none.

"There's a game called 'ring-knife' that we used to play when I was a kid. You use your jackknife. You draw a circle on the ground, see, and you place small stones in it—so far apart—then you stand back and toss your knife. Your knife has to stick upright in the ground—that means that you have to miss those stones. Each time that you succeed, you get to move back a pace. If your knife doesn't stand up, you have to start over. Winner is the one who can tally up the most paces back. At the end of the time limit each player uses his best score. Want to try it?"

I felt that I was pretty good with my knife and the game sounded kind of fun so I agreed.

By now we had walked together onto the back porch. Auntie Lou and Hiram were sippin' lemonade and chattin' about something. Hiram looked down-right pleased with himself, but Auntie Lou still hadn't quite been able to shake off her look of confusion.

Gramps stopped to exchange a few words.

"Joshua and I are going to have us a little game here."

We went on. Gramps drew out the circle in the dirt, and we each placed three smooth stones inside it.

It was easy for the first few paces, but it got tougher as we went along. We made the first game jest ten minutes. I had tallied up eleven paces as my best score and Gramps ten.

As I was retrievin' our knives for another go at it, Gramps did a rather funny thing. He pulled out his purse and handed me a dime. His voice was low.

"Been meaning to give you this. When you go to town next time, I'd like you to pick out a good fishhook for me—one that you think would have those fish squirming for a chance at it."

Seemed funny to me that Gramps would be thinkin' of fishhooks at such a time, but I nodded and put the dime in the pocket of my pants. I don't know jest what brought my head up at that particular time, but as my glance went to the porch I saw Hiram lookin' at us. I thought nothing about it except the usual fear and anger at seein' him there with Lou. I handed Gramps his knife. He carefully cleaned the blade of his knife and we started a new game. This one ended again as Gramps consulted his pocket watch. I bettered my score a bit that game, and Gramps ended up two paces behind me.

"Been thinking, Joshua," he said as we retrieved our knives, "maybe you'd best get two hooks so that we'll each have one."

Hadn't realized jest how "hooked" on fishin' Gramps was after only one trip to the crik. He took out his change purse and handed me another dime. He jiggled the coins as though he was having trouble locating jest the right one. I dumbly put the dime in my pocket knowin' that it was more money than I needed for two hooks. I'd git the best ones that I could find and give Gramps back his change.

Gramps raised his voice. I was only a few paces from him—but he did have his back to me, so maybe he thought I had walked away.

"Okay, Joshua, that's enough practicing. Let's get into the *real* game now."

It was then that I noticed Hiram edgin' his way off the porch and over toward us. Gramps stood there examining his knife and cleaning the dirt from the blade. Hiram came in closer.

"Interestin' game," he finally said.

"Ever play ring-knife?" Gramps asked.

"Nope."

"Know the rules?"

"I've been watchin'."

Gramps sensed his interest.

"Want to join us?"

Hiram grinned then.

"Sure would like to give it a try."

He pulled out his pocket knife and checked the tip for sharpness.

"We were just about to start the big one. Go ahead and take a few practice throws."

Gramps hauled out his watch and studied the time while Hiram threw. He looked pretty good with a knife.

Gramps let him have three throws from varyin' distances.

"Okay," he said, watching his timepiece carefully as though it had to be the exact second for startin', "Joshua, you start." A pause, then a flash of the watch in his hand—"Go."

I threw—my knife stuck upright. The game was on.

"Hiram," Gramps said with a nod.

Hiram threw. His knife held firm. Gramps took extra time as he threw, as though the game had suddenly become very important. I sensed the change and it made me feel that maybe we *had* jest been foolin' around before. Hiram seemed to sense it, too, and I could see the excitement in his face.

Gramps measured the distance, judged the position of the stones, studied his knife carefully for balance and threw. His knife stood upright and I heard him sigh with satisfaction.

We all picked up our knives and backed up a pace. The rounds went much more slowly now. Gramps seemed to set the pace. He played so differently that it was hard to believe we were playin' the same game that he had first introduced me to. Round by round we studied, threw, took our paces backward and retrieved our knives. Uncle Charlie and Grandpa came to watch for a while with anxious looks on their faces; but seein' our deep involvement, they finally shrugged and went away.

I'll say this for Hiram. When he takes to a game he does it with his whole heart and soul. I'd hardly seen a man so keen about playin' a game. Gramps was serious about it, too; he played slowly and carefully, but he seemed to have a calmness about him that Hiram was lackin'.

All the rest of the afternoon we played. Pace by pace we stepped back until we were so far away that we could hardly see the circle—then we'd go back to start over.

I moved backward and forward more often than the others. It was hard to believe that I had actually managed to beat Gramps in my first two games. Beginner's luck—I guess.

Hiram was in a sweat. It stood out in little drops on his forehead, and it wasn't due to the pleasant fall day.

Lou had long ago taken her leave. I had spotted her heading toward the crik with a book in her hand. Uncle Charlie and Grandpa paced back and forth on the back porch, scowlin' and upset, but the game went on.

Gramps and Hiram hung together pace by pace. Occasionally Gramps consulted his pocket watch, rattlin' its chain rather unnecessarily as he did so; then he'd shake his head to indicate that time still wasn't up and we'd go at it again.

Frankly, I was getting rather tired of the game, but Hiram didn't seem to be. Gramps was one pace behind him and Hiram seemed determined to keep it that way.

Gramps looked at his watch again.

"One minute to go. This will be our last throw."

Hiram chewed his lip. They were now both standing together at their record distance. If they both made it, it could end up a tie. Of course I was pullin' for Gramps. I was so far behind that I didn't even count anymore.

Hiram almost looked in pain as he lined up for his last toss. I thought that he was never goin' to let go of that knife, but he finally did; the blade flashed as it arced through the air. It hit the ground with a soft sound; it had cleared the stones—it quivered as it held upright. Hiram looked like he would whoop, but he didn't. He whipped out his handkerchief and wiped his brow.

It was Gramps' turn now. He took his time and aimed carefully. A calmness still showed in his face. I would have loved to put a toe to Hiram's knife. I was hopin' for at least a tie—that would take the sting out of the situation.

Hiram was almost jumpin' out of his shoes; I was afraid that his agitation would disturb Gramps' concentration. I sent him a scowl but he didn't even notice.

Gramps' knife finally left his hand and made a clean, quick flight toward the circle. It seemed that the whole of me went flyin' with that knife. No one stirred—or even breathed. I waited for the soft sound of the blade slippin' into the dirt, but instead there was a sharp "clink" and a clatter. Gramps' knife had hit the largest rock.

Hiram whooped—I wanted to kick him. Poor Gramps—after playin' so hard and so long. But Gramps was a much better loser than I was on his behalf. He turned to Hiram with a good-natured smile.

"Great game for a novice," he said, extending his hand.

I didn't know what "novice" meant, but I sure did know the meanin' I'd put to it.

Hiram was still so excited that he could hardly even shake Gramps' hand proper-like. I wondered how a supposed grown man could get so riled up about winnin' a simple little game—even if it did take all afternoon to play.

"Congratulations," I heard Gramps sayin'. "You sure are one terrific ring-knife player."

Hiram was still bouncin' around and shaking Gramps' hand vigorously.

"How much did I win?" he blurted out.

"Win?" Gramps looked dumbfounded—I knew I was. Uncle Charlie and Grandpa, who had come on over, looked a little surprised too.

"Yeah. . ." Hiram's glee began to fade from his face. "Don't ya—"

"I never played a game for money in my life." Gramps looked offended. "That's gambling. If a game can't be played for the sheer joy of the playing, then leave it alone, I always say."

"But you gave Josh—"

"I gave Josh a couple of dimes to buy fishhooks the next time he goes to town. He and I plan to do some fishing before he has to go back to school."

Hiram had added an embarrassed look to his one of disappointment. He cleared his throat and cleaned his knife with his eyes turned from everyone.

Lou, who had returned, luckily chose that moment to announce that coffee was ready, so we all trooped into the house. Her timin' couldn't have been better. The air was a mite heavy, though I still couldn't rightly understand the situation fully.

Hiram left as soon as he had swallowed the last of his cake and washed it down with coffee. He thanked Uncle Charlie rather weakly for the invitation, but he kept his eyes away from Lou's, even as he mumbled his thanks for the dinner. He also avoided Gramps. It was rather comical watchin' him scuttle around hardly knowin' which way to look.

Uncle Charlie went with Hiram to get his team and the big bays fairly thundered out of our yard. Uncle Charlie returned. Lou was busy clearin' the table; no one jumped up to protest her activity and suggest that she rest herself.

Gramps grinned at me sort of silly and gave a quick wink.

He turned to Uncle Charlie. He shook his head slowly as though he was really at a loss to understand it all.

"Your friend seemed like such a nice young man, Charles. I just can hardly believe that he would be a gambler. It's a shame, a downright shame!"

I had to run outside before I busted out laughin'.

Chapter 12

Fall Days

Uncle Charlie was going to town for some binder twine, and Gramps decided that he'd ride along with him. I ached to go too, but I had too many chores that needed finishing. I still had those two dimes that Gramps had given me, and I could hardly wait to check over the fishhooks at Kirk's. I offered them back to Gramps, thinkin' that he might like to buy the hooks himself, but he said that I knew more about such things.

I worked with rather draggin' feet. It seemed strange and lonesome somehow without Gramps there to sort of spur me on.

After dinner I had some free time, so I got out my fishin' tackle and cleaned up my hooks. I nearly stuck myself with one of them; Auntie Lou got all excited and said that I'd better put them away. My handlin' fishhooks always made her nervous.

I went out to split wood. I had made quite a stack before I finally heard the wagon comin'. I slammed the axe head into the choppin' block and sauntered into the kitchen.

"They're comin'."

"Are they?"

"Yep."

There was a pause. Auntie Lou was havin' a few rare minutes with one of those mail-order catalogues. She kept right on lookin'.

"Coffee ready?"

She looked up, her fine eyebrows archin'.

"You wantin' coffee?"

"Not me—Gramps and Uncle Charlie. Jest thought that they might kinda like a cup—or juice or somethin'."

Lou smiled and laid aside the fascinating pages.

"So you're hungry, are ya, Josh?"

It wasn't what I meant, but I didn't care that Lou took me wrong. By the time the men came in from the barn, Lou had cut some molasses cake, and the coffee was about ready to boil. At my place was a tall glass of milk.

Gramps passed close to me and placed his hand on my shoulder. I sorta felt like pressin' myself against him and waggin' my tail.

"How'd chores go?"

"Fine. I got done in pretty good time. Even cleaned up my fishhooks."

"I was going to take a look at the hooks in the general store just to see what they carried, but I didn't get around to it."

I wondered what Gramps had been doin' with all of his time in town that he didn't even find time to look at fishhooks. Uncle Charlie entered.

"Saw a little notice posted in the general store that might interest you, Josh."

I looked at Uncle Charlie, wonderin' what a notice in Kirk's store would have to do with me. I didn't need to wonder long.

"Says big an' bold-like, 'School starts Monday.' "

Uncle Charlie lifted one finger as though pointin' out each one of the big black-lettered words.

My face must have dropped, because Uncle Charlie laughed, and Gramps seemed to look about as disappointed as I felt.

"So soon?" he questioned Uncle Charlie.

Uncle Charlie nodded.

"Harvest is early this year and most folks are gittin' near done. Saw Mr. T. Smith in town. He says a few hours today will finish him. Made arrangements myself for the threshing crew to come in on Thursday. Jest the little bits of greenfeed that Dan is workin' on today and all our cuttin' will be done. The other fields are stooked and dryin' real fast. They'll all be ready for sure come Thursday."

"Well, I best be gittin'."

He got up from the table and then seemed to remember something. He pulled a small brown bag from a shirt pocket and handed it to Auntie Lou. When Uncle Charlie went to town he always came home with a few gums, licorice sticks, or peppermint drops. He winked at Auntie Lou.

"Ya might even share one or two with Josh, iffen he behaves himself."

He flipped his hat onto his head and was gone.

"Next Monday. . ." Gramps repeated. "That means we have to do our fishing this week, Joshua. Think we can manage it?"

I was now doubly glad for the nice pile of firewood that I had stacked outside.

"Tomorrow," I said. "We'll count on tomorrow. I'll git out there right now and add to that woodpile before I have to start sloppin' the pigs."

As I hurried out I thought on how Uncle Charlie had brought some good news and some bad news. Wasn't hard to decide which side of the board the word about school startin' would fit. The good news was concernin' the threshin' crew. Threshin' was one of my favorite events of the year.

It usually started early in the morning. Always as I rushed about the early mornin' chores, I found myself listenin' for the chug-chug of the big threshin' rig coming up the road. Before long it would be devourin' bundles and spittin' out golden grain from one spout and blowin' high a stream of straw from another.

The first few hours were spent in settin' up the threshin' machine. After it was positioned and seemed in readiness, the giant steam tractor was started. The long flappin' belt began to whirl, and it in turn activated all manner of movin' things on the threshin' machine. At first all of the gears were in slow motion, grindin' and howlin' as they seemed to protest at bein' put to work again. The man who owned the machine never sat still for a minute. He ran back and forth, around and around, checkin' here and checkin' there. After he had looked and listened to his heart's content, he left the big machine idlin' and came to the house for breakfast.

I sat at breakfast strainin' to be the first to hear the jangle of harness and the clankin' of steel-rimmed wheels as they ground their way over the hard-packed road.

There would be at least five or six teams in all. Sometimes they stopped at the house, while other times they went right on down to the field.

When the teams arrived, the machine operator would swallow the last of his coffee and make his way back to his rig; there he'd circle and listen and open little side doors, look in and poke a bit.

Finally when the sun had been up long enough to dry the grain bundles, the lead team moved out. A couple of extra men rode along, and they would fork on the bundles as the team moved slowly down the field, stoppin' and startin' at the command of their owner who worked along beside the wagon, pitchin' bundles with the other two fellas.

They wouldn't bring in a full rack, this first load jest bein' for testin'; as soon as they had enough to test they returned to the threshin' machine. That's when things really came to life. The levers were pulled, throwin' the big machines into full motion. The steam engine roared and trembled, shootin' out gray-black smoke. The gears clashed and banged on the threshin' machine as it picked up its pace. It seemed to rock and stomp like an angry dragon. I often marveled that it didn't rock itself right on down the field. Guess the owner thought the same, because he always packed rocks up tight against the steel wheels.

At the nod of the machine operator, the team moved in close to the machine, and the bundle pitchers went into motion, too, tossin' the bundles onto the belts that carried them up and fed them into the belly of the big machine.

That was where the miracle took place. Instead of comin' out as they had gone in, or even chopped and mutilated, the grain spout soon began to let streams of clean grain pour into the box of the wagon that sat carefully teamed in beneath it. A small cloud puffed from the spout that blew away the straw; the cloud grew and grew, becoming shimmering gold and silver flashes as the sun hit the flying particles.

I always stood in awe. It never ceased to amaze me, this sudden and well-ordered change.

If the threshed sample was satisfactory—the men decided this by lookin', handlin' and even chewin' the grain—the waitin' teams were given the signal and away they went, down the field, eager to be on with the job.

There were other things that I liked about threshin' time, too—like seein' the grain grow deeper and deeper in the wagon box. It was then transported to the grain bin where it was shovelled off with rhythmic swings of scrunch—whoosh, scrunch—whoosh. It smelled good, too, though sometimes the dust made you sneeze. Then there was the fun of chasin' mice that came skitterin' out from the grain shocks.

I loved the food too. Harvest time always meant a well-loaded table, for harvesters worked hard and needed hearty meals. We always got help for Auntie Lou at harvest time. It was jest too much for one woman to handle all the work of feedin' the harvest crew alone.

As I chopped wood, I looked forward to Thursday. I could hardly wait for the sound of the teams movin' in.

Gramps and I did manage to sneak in that fishin' trip on Wednesday. My only sorrow was that I hadn't been able to get into town to pick out some new hooks. Still, my old favorites seemed to have done okay in the past, so I trusted that they would again work well.

Gramps carried his pole and the lunch pail, while I handled my pole, a can of worms and dirt, and an old coat for Gramps to sit on. We decided to try a different hole this time—one a little further upstream. There was a swell log there, made perfect for sittin'—with the help of a little padding—and a couple of sturdy trees right behind it for anyone who preferred to lean against them to rest his back.

Gramps was a quick learner. He strung his own hook and had it in the water even before I did. He jiggled it occasionally—jest enough—and we settled in to talk as we waited for a fish to strike.

"You know, Joshua," said Gramps with a bit of a chuckle, "I've been thinking that I've pretty well got it made."

I looked at him sort of puzzled.

"Meanin'?"

"You know," he explained, "I think that I've hit the best years of a man's life."

I still wasn't followin'.

He chuckled softly as though he really had a good laugh on the rest of the scurryin' world.

"Take you now," he explained. "Sure you've got your delights—your fishing, your lack of adult worries; but you work hard, too."

I was glad that Gramps had noticed.

"And then you've got your schooling, like it or not—and I hope that you do like it. But you still have to go.

"Your Grandpa and your Uncle Charlie, they have men's work and men's worries. Takes most of their time and energy to just keep up with things.

"But *me* now. . . ," he sighed a contented sigh and leaned back smugly against the warm tree trunk. "Me—I don't have to go to school, privilege that it is, or even chore if I don't feel like it. No one expects me to hurry around with a pitchfork or a scoop-shovel in my hand. No one raises an eyebrow if I want to lay in a bit in the morning or crawl off to bed at a kid's bedtime at night. I don't have to make tough decisions—like which spring calves to sell and which to keep, or what crop to plant in which field, or whether to fix the old plow again, or buy a new one. No sirree, Joshua. I've got it made."

I was gettin' the point. I'd never even considered that there were advantages to being old. Gramps clearly had found some.

He grinned at me with humor dancin' in his blue eyes.

"Just eat, and sleep and look after the old man."

It sounded pretty good all right, but not quite accurate for Gramps. I kept gettin' pictures of him feeding the chickens, pumping water for the stock or toting wood. I also saw him with his shirt sleeves rolled up peeling vegetables, or drying dishes or even sweeping up the kitchen floor.

Maybe he was right in a way. Maybe he didn't *have* to do those things; but knowin' Gramps, I had the feelin' that as long as he could still totter, he'd be doin' what he could to lighten someone's load. Guess he liked it that way. He was a great old guy, my Gramps.

"Yes sirree," he said again, bobbin' his line, "best part of a man's life. If I had Mama here it would be just perfect."

He started tellin' me all about Great-grandma then—how he'd met her when he was only nineteen and decided right off that she was the girl for him. He went on, through their life spent together, rememberin' little things that probably seemed insignificant when they happened. He didn't talk about what had happened after she had gone, but knowin' Great-grandma, from the tone of Gramps' voice and the descriptions he had given, it was easy for me to feel his loss. I didn't have to wonder how he felt—I'd lost family too.

We fished in silence for a while and then decided that it was time for lunch. I was beginning to worry that I had chosen the wrong fishin' hole for the day; I so much wanted to see Gramps catch another one.

We had jest lifted cold chicken drumsticks from the pail when I sensed a commotion in the water; sure enough, Gramps had one on. He jumped up, dropped his chicken and went whoopin' and yellin' down the bank. I joined him. We were shoutin' and dancin' and callin' to one another. By the time we landed the fish and got back to the lunch pail, the ants were already havin' a picnic of the dropped chicken. I tossed it, ants and all, off to the side to try to discourage the old ants-up-the-pant-leg trick.

Gramps had jest landed one of the nicest sunnies that I'd ever seen taken from the crik, and I could hardly swallow I was so excited. I even forgot to hope that I would have equal luck; if we would have had to pack up and head for home right then and there, I would have been perfectly happy. I did catch one before we had to leave, though it wasn't as fine as Gramps'.

We went home happy.

"Glad we were able to fit this day in, Joshua," Gramps said.

"Me too."

"You're good company, Joshua."

No one had ever said anything like that to me before.

"Hope that you didn't mind an old man sharing some memories."

I looked at him. " 'Course not."

He put a hand on my hair and ruffled it the way that grown-ups have a habit of doin'.

We walked on. Shucks! Why should I mind sharin' Gramps' memories? Especially since I didn't have any of my own anyway.

That strange twistin' hurt squeezed somewhere in my insides again. I started to walk a little faster.

Chapter 13

Threshin'

Thursday came. We were all able to let out the breath that we'd been holdin'. There's always the threat of bad weather movin' in on a threshin' operation. It delays the plans and makes big men sweat with worry over something that they have no power to do a thing about. Used to be I'd pray for days on end before threshin', pleadin' with the Lord to favor us with fittin' weather. Last year a bad storm moved in on us in spite of my prayers, so this year I decided that I would jest leave the Lord on His own.

I rose earlier than usual. I wanted my chores out of the way so that I could catch every bit of action that I possibly could.

As I looked out on the clear autumn mornin', I did have a stirrin' of thankfulness, even if I did hold back the desire to express it.

I was bringin' Bossie in from the field when I first heard the distant chug-chuggin'. I hoped that the sound of the comin' machine didn't fill Bossie with the same wild excitement that it did me—or her milk wouldn't be worth much that mornin'.

I milked hurriedly and was jest finishing when the slow-movin' tractor, with the big black thresher in tow, turned up our lane.

Grandpa and Uncle Charlie went out to meet Mr. Wilkes, the man who operated the machine.

Mr. Wilkes had been runnin' that machine for all of the harvests that I could remember. Neither he nor the machine looked shiny-new anymore, but they did look like they belonged together. To Mr. Wilkes the machine was not only his bread and butter but his friend and companion as well. He took great pride in it. Mr. Wilkes didn't bother to plant crops of his own anymore. In fact, he share-cropped his land with Mr. T. Smith. By farmin' Mr. Wilkes' fields, Mr. T. Smith was almost certain to be the first man on the list for threshin' come fall.

Mr. Wilkes depended on the money he'd make each autumn from tourin' from farm to farm rentin' out the services of himself and his magic machine. The two things that worried him most were drought and fires. His was the only thresher available in our area and nobody seemed to think it could be any other way.

I hurried the pail of milk to the house.

Already Mrs. Corbin and her daughter, SueAnn, were there to help Auntie Lou. I don't believe that Lou shared my excitement about harvest time. She always looked as though she found the kitchen a bit crowded with other women scurryin' around. I think that she would have enjoyed spending the day with SueAnn, but Mrs. Corbin was a rather busy, take-over sort of person.

I handed Auntie Lou the milk pail and headed back for the barn on the run. By now Mr. Wilkes was movin' the black-puffin' machine into the wheat field jest beyond the house. It would take him some time to make sure that everything was set and ready to go.

I rushed through the remainder of the early mornin' chores and managed to get out to the field in time for Mr. Wilkes' final pre-breakfast inspection. Boy, did I envy him. To be able to work with all those gears and pulleys and movin' parts must be something.

I stood watchin' the trembling sides of the big thresher, trembling a little myself. Later, when she really started to roll, she wouldn't jest tremble; she'd shake and heave.

Mr. Wilkes must have been satisfied, for he put the tractor on a low idle and turned to Grandpa and Uncle Charlie, indicating that he was ready for breakfast.

That mornin' I passed up the porridge and instead enjoyed bacon, eggs, fried potatoes, pancakes and bran muffins. Only at harvest time did we have all of those things on the self-same mornin'.

The man-talk flew all around me, and from a little further away came the higher pitched, soft voices of the womenfolk as they worked over the stove, flippin' pancakes and turnin' bacon.

Gramps seemed to catch the feelin' of things. I knew that he had never been a part of threshin' time before, and I felt that life had kinda cheated him. I wouldn't have traded harvest for—well—even for a circus. I guess harvest is a kind of circus all its own, with action and excitement and noise—even trained animals. When you watched a harvest team worm its way down the field between the grain stooks without any man ever touchin' a rein, then you knew that they were well trained. I sure was looking forward to all of the action.

Before breakfast ended, I heard the jingle of harness. Without even thinkin' to excuse myself, I ran to the window.

It was Mr. T. Smith and his team of bays. Those horses were thought to be the finest team that ever turned up at a threshin' site—at least Mr. T. thought so. He was continually tellin' the fact to everyone else on the crew, much to the annoyance of some of the other farmers.

"When they're told to stand, they stand," Mr. T. would say; "never move a hair or flick an eyelash. An' when they move down the field, they always keep thet perfect five-foot distance between the side of the rack and the stooks. Never an inch more or less. Gives a man jest the right space fer workin' without costin' him a bit of extra time or energy in throwin' bundles." Mr. T. spent every lunch break and every mealtime braggin' about his team.

I should have known that Mr. T. would be first in. He always was. He never refused an invitation to sit up to table and have a little breakfast either; but as Mr. T. was a hardworkin' man and always earned his way at harvest time, no one minded stokin' his furnace before he left for the field.

By the time Mr. T. had finished his breakfast, tellin' of his bays between each mouthful, other wagons were arriving. Six teams came in, along with three extra men who would work as field pitchers, spike pitchers and bundle clean-up men—no one wanted even a few bundles left layin' in the field for mouse feed.

Grandpa and Uncle Charlie would man the wagons to be filled with the new grain; turn by turn they'd unload it in the grain bins.

All totaled we had twelve men out there: Mr. Wilkes, six drivers, three extra pitchers, and Grandpa and Uncle Charlie.

The sun was up and shining brightly. Mr. Wilkes made a final turn around the rumbling machine and nodded his satisfaction. He gave Mr. T. the signal, and he and Burt Thomas and Barkley Shaw moved between a long line of stooks. They jest forked on enough bundles to make a decent test batch and returned to the machine. Mr. Wilkes pulled the lever that started the long belt flappin' faster and the threshin' machine began its dusty dance. Mr. T. drove the team of bays right alongside the carrier; sure enough, they never flickered an ear at all the snortin', sneezin', stompin' and rockin' of the threshin' rig. You'd have thought that they were standin' contentedly in their own stalls.

As soon as the machine was rattlin' to Mr. Wilke's satisfaction, he waved a hand at Mr. T., and bundles were fed rhythmically unto the conveyor. Up they slowly climbed and I imagined angry clickin' teeth gnashin' at them as they disappeared behind the canvas curtain.

I ran around to the other end. I wanted to be sure to be on hand when the first trickle of grain started leavin' the spout. It soon came and Grandpa and Uncle Charlie both grabbed for handfuls. They felt it, eyed it, and then each put a few kernels in their mouth. They chewed silently for a moment, watchin' each other's eyes for the message that would be reflected there. Finally Uncle Charlie nodded and Grandpa returned the nod. Mr. Wilkes, who had been feelin' and chewin' too, took the nods as his signal and went back to wave the wagons out.

Away they rolled, each man determined to prove his brawn by bein' the first one to fill his wagon.

On this trip Burt Thomas went with Mr. P. Smith; Mr. Smith had broken his leg many years before and walked with a bad limp because of a poor settin' of the broken bone.

Barkley Shaw went with Mr. Peterson who really was gettin' a little too old for the threshin' crew. No one would have told him so though, him seemin' to look forward to harvest each fall. They usually put a younger man on with him—sort of off-hand and matter-a-fact—and old Mr. Peterson now seemed to jest expect it.

Joey Smith walked between two wagons, throwin' bundles on one or the other, depending on which wagon the stook was closest to. Later he would take a shift as spike-pitcher, feedin' the bundles into the thresher.

I looked around from all the action and noticed that Gramps was standin' there fascinated by it all, too. It was difficult to talk—the machine made too much noise; but we grinned at one another in the commotion and the excitement.

The first teams back began to throw the bundles onto the feeder, and we watched as they were gulped up by the hungry machine. I motioned for Gramps to come with me. I led him around to the grain wagon where Uncle Charlie sat watchin' the stream of grain fall from the spout. Occasionally he'd reach out with his shovel and scrape the peak off the grain that piled in the wagon box. Gramps watched, his blue eyes sparklin'. He reached a hand into the box and let several handfuls of the wheat trickle through his fingers. He seemed to like the feel of it. Uncle Charlie grinned and nodded—I knew what he meant; this year's crop was of good quality.

I nudged Gramps and pointed a finger at the spewin' straw. Gramps lifted his eyes from the wagon box. He stood watchin' the straw sail out in a big arc, twistin' and turnin' and catchin' the sunlight.

The teams moved back and forth in the field, the men steadily working along beside them; the big machine heaved and snorted, the grain fell in a steady stream and the straw blew, light and glitterin', in the clear mornin' air.

Gramps leaned close to me.

"Better than a circus!" he yelled in my ear.

I grinned. I had wanted to hear that.

Later in the mornin' the ladies came with the mornin' lunch. The machine was idled down to give it some coolin' time, too.

The men drank pails of cold water to cool them off, followed by hot coffee to heat them up again—never could make any sense out of that. They also wolfed down large amounts of sandwiches and cookies.

The break was used for other things, too. Mr. Wilkes poked around and around his machine again, Mr. T. took the opportunity to brag about the bays, Mr. P. Smith propped up his bad leg on a couple of bundles to give it a rest, and Mr. Peterson stretched right out on the ground. He passed up an extra cup of coffee for a couple of winks.

It was quite obvious how the younger fellas preferred spendin' the few extra minutes. They seemed to be playin' a little game of seein' who could git a bit of attention from Auntie Lou. I saw Grandpa and Uncle Charlie watchin' them. Gramps watched, too, only I caught him smilin' in a secret way as though he was maybe rememberin' again.

Joey Smith drank cup after cup of coffee poured by Auntie Lou's hands. I was told later that Joey didn't even care for coffee.

Barkley Shaw was jest a little over-noisy and energetic. I think Grandpa decided about then that it was time for Barkley's shift at the feeder as spike-pitcher.

Burt Thomas was more agreeable, but not too subtle, makin' comments on how good the cookies were and "did you make them yerself," and all that.

I got kinda fed up on the whole thing and went off to see if I could find a few mice to chase.

At dinnertime Gramps and I would be eatin' with the womenfolk after the dozen men had been fed. It was all that

Auntie Lou could do to squeeze twelve full-grown men around our kitchen table, even with the extension on. When the time came for the noon meal, I didn't even go in with the menfolk. I sat on a choppin' block out at the woodpile and watched and listened as they sloshed water at the outside basins and jostled one another good-naturedly.

When they had gone in I still sat there. I'd already had my fill of Mr. T.'s bays and the sheep-eyes made by love-struck dummies. In a few minutes Gramps joined me.

"Kind of fun isn't it, Joshua?"

I caught the spirit again and we sat on our blocks and talked threshin'.

After the last of the men had left the house, we waited to let the women have enough time to clear the table of the dirty dishes and make it ready for us. While we waited we watched the men rehitchin' the horses that had also had their water and feed durin' the noon break. As the last team moved out, Auntie Lou called us to come in.

I was hungry in spite of all that I had eaten at morning lunch, and I enjoyed every mouthful of the huge spread. Gramps seemed to be enjoyin' it, too. His appetite had picked up considerably since he had joined us.

Several times during our meal SueAnn giggled. I wasn't used to hearin' a girl giggle like that. Auntie Lou never did. Either she laughed softly or she gave a full-throated chuckle—never did she giggle. I finally took time out from my eatin' to look at SueAnn. Her face was flushed and she appeared right excited about something. I guessed then that she had probably gotten a big kick out of servin' the meal to the men—especially the younger ones. She giggled again and I found it to my dislikin'. I looked over at Auntie Lou.

Her face was a bit flushed, too, and her eyes danced like they had taken and given some merry teasin'. It shook me up a mite. I tried to ask myself, "Why not?" but all I could get was, "Why?" Still, Auntie Lou was young and pretty; she could get the full attention of the young men, and I guess it was kinda natural that she might sort of enjoy it some. Even so, I was glad that she wasn't silly-actin' and giggly about it. I couldn't tolerate a gigglin' girl. At least Auntie Lou carried herself with some dignity.

I forked the last of my lemon pie into my mouth in a hurry to get away from SueAnn. I could hardly manage " 'Scuse me please," through the mouthful, but before anyone could protest I slipped from the table. There were chores that needed doing and wood that needed chopping before I'd be free to go to the field for a while again. I wanted to make the most of each moment.

The wood chopping seemed to take forever. I finished jest in time to walk out to the field with the two girls who were taking out the lunch. Auntie Lou collared me to carry a couple pails of water, or I would have run on ahead.

The men had been watchin' for the women to appear and didn't take long in gatherin' for the refreshments. The cool water was the most popular item at the outset, but when the men had quenched their thirst, they turned eagerly to the sandwiches, cake and coffee.

Things were movin' along real well. Mr. T. was horse-braggin', Mr. P. was restin' his leg, and Mr. Wilkes was inspectin' his beloved machine, a sandwich in one hand and a coffee cup in the other. Auntie Lou was doin' the pouring duties. SueAnn was passing out the sandwiches and cake.

Barkley Shaw and Joe Smith sauntered up to the girls—again. There was something about the way they approached those girls that gave me the feelin' that something was a-brewin'. I wasn't wrong. All of a sudden Barkley thrust his coffee cup at Joey yellin', "Hold this! hold this!" and he started jumpin' around in a circle, clutchin' and tearin' at his pant leg, hootin' and stompin' and carryin' on something awful.

"What's wrong? What's wrong?" yelled Joey, desperately tryin' to keep both full cups from spillin'. The two girls stood there, their eyes wide with wonder, or horror, I wasn't sure which.

"Got a mouse up my pant leg!" hollered Barkley and continued to dance around and slap at his denimed leg. At the word "mouse" SueAnn turned into a wild thing. She heaved the sandwiches that she had been holdin' and with a shriek of pure terror looked frantically for some place to crawl onto. The only thing at hand was Mr. P.'s two bundles under his leg. SueAnn jumped, up the full ten inches onto the sheaves, barely missin' Mr. P.'s poor achin' leg.

She continued to squeal and screech, swishin' her skirts and stompin' 'til she had nearly threshed out those two sheaves herself.

Barkley Shaw stopped his dance and began hootin' and laughin' at SueAnn. Joey set down the coffee cups, and they leaned against one another, slappin' their thighs and poundin' each other's back as they howled with laughter.

Auntie Lou smiled a tiny smile and went over to pour coffee for the older men; she completely ignored the two young bucks who were still cacklin' away about their smart-aleck joke.

Mr. Peterson reached out and reclaimed a sandwich from the stubble. He blew away a small piece of straw or two and began to eat as calmly as though he ate off the ground every day. Gramps retrieved the rest of the dropped sandwiches.

It took SueAnn several minutes to realize that it had all been a hoax; even then she was reluctant to come down from her spot on the bundles. Mr. P. mumbled and moved his leg elsewhere. Mr. Wilkes gave a nod that meant fun and games were over and it was time for everyone to get back to work. The expression on his face had not changed so much as a flicker through the entire episode.

Slowly everyone returned to his team, Joey and Barkley still holdin' their sides and the other young fellas givin' an occasional chuckle as well. They had enjoyed it tremendously.

The girls gathered the cups and pails together. SueAnn looked red and angry. She hadn't found any part of it the least bit amusin'. She was still sputterin' a little when she and Auntie Lou headed for the house.

The rest of the day seemed rather uneventful after that. The men came in dusty and hungry for the evening meal. They first watered and fed their tired horses and then came to wash.

The threshin' machine had to be moved to our other field

for the next day's work, so Mr. Wilkes didn't come for supper until he'd done jest that.

Everyone was tired, so there wasn't much talk. Every now and then one of the young fellas would look at SueAnn and grin. She pretended to be terribly upset with Barkley, but I wondered if she wasn't jest a little pleased over all of the attention. She'd lift her chin a little higher and give Barkley a poisonous glare each time that she looked at him. This would jest make the boys laugh even harder. Anyway, I figured that her dark looks and flippin' skirts sure beat her gigglin'.

About the only older man that seemed rested enough to talk was Mr. T. Smith. He was busy takin' a survey to see who had noticed how his bays had performed. Not many men had, but that jest gave Mr. T. an excuse to inform them. Most of the men looked unimpressed, but no one bothered to stop him.

They had made good progress on the first day. It looked like the weather would hold good for the next day as well. That would finish our crop. Grandpa and Uncle Charlie didn't sow as much grain now as they used to. They sowed more greenfeed and hay and fed our cattle instead. Grandpa said that that's where the money was, and even though Uncle Charlie never argued and went right along with it, I always got the feelin' that he somehow didn't quite agree.

The next day's threshin' started out pretty much the same. The teams arrived, Mr. Wilkes started his machine, and things swung into motion again.

Later in the mornin' Cullum Lewis noticed me hangin' around and asked if I'd like to go for a load with him. Cullum Lewis was a big fella for his age, and he drove a team of his own. This was already his fourth year on a threshin' crew, so I guessed he probably knew all about it.

As he forked bundles, he let me chase mice to my heart's content. When he had the rack piled high, we crawled up and settled in on the load for the return trip to the machine. Cullum even let me hold the reins. We didn't talk much. He asked me one or two questions about Auntie Lou, like, did she have a regular beau and did I think she might like one? I answered "no" to both questions and Cullum dropped the matter. He was rather a likable guy in a way, and I couldn't help but think that if ever Auntie Lou should change her mind—and I s'posed that she might—then Cullum might not be such a bad choice. He'd sure be a heap better than either Jedd Rawleigh or Hiram Woxley.

During the dinner hour Mr. Wilkes had to move the machine again. He wouldn't even stop to eat. The men took their time about dinner, knowin' that Mr. Wilkes wouldn't be ready to go for a while.

At the table Joey Smith asked Barkley Shaw if he'd had anymore trouble with mice—SueAnn refused to serve them tea. That didn't bother the boys any. I got the feelin' that they preferred Auntie Lou servin' them anyway. Mrs. Corbin didn't pay any attention to the goings on. She was a simple, no-nonsense person, and I don't suppose that she ever saw humor in anything. Gramps was takin' it all in though. I could see his mustache twitch every now and then, and I knew that he was hidin' a smile.

As the men left the house, Mr. T. was busy braggin' about the bays again.

"Most dependable horses I ever had," he was saying, "an' I've had me some good ones. Nothin' would spook thet pair— not the devil hisself."

I saw Barkley exchange a quick look with Burt Thomas.

The final field was the furthest from the house. When it came time for the afternoon coffee break, the girls rode out to the field with Uncle Charlie in the empty grain wagon. They would catch a ride home with Grandpa in a full one.

The menfolk were feelin' extra good because they knew that they were near the end. They would finish the field and thus our threshin', jest in time for supper.

The older men settled themselves here and there on the ground, enjoyin' the coffee and sandwiches. They discussed the year's crops—not jest on our land, but the neighbor's as well. Everyone knew that the grain was a good quality but the yield was down. We hadn't had as much rain as we should have had, and the wheat jest didn't produce like it usually did. Still, it was a fair crop and it was nearly all in the bin, so no one at our house was complainin'.

The young fellas teased and pushed as usual. Cullum Lewis was the quietest one of the lot. I watched him as his eyes followed Auntie Lou. Mentally, I fought for him and against him at the same time. Auntie Lou didn't seem to notice him at all—but then maybe she did. I don't know.

I noticed Barkley and Burt wander apart from the rest, and the next time I looked for them they were gone. I paid no mind to it and went back to my ginger cake.

Mr. T.'s team had been restin' in the shade of the trees at the edge of the field, heads down, quietly and patiently standin', even though they had no rein to tie them. The rack carried a full load—Mr. T. would be the next man up to the machine.

At the signal from Mr. Wilkes the men pulled themselves up from the ground and brushed the loose stubble from their pants. Mr. P. picked up his two bundles and tossed them up on his rack so that they wouldn't be missed. He wouldn't be needin' them anymore.

Mr. T. stepped up on the tongue of his wagon and grabbed hold of the rack without even reachin' for the reins, which he would pick up on his way into the machine if he felt that he needed them. He hollered "giddup" to the bays and began to climb leisurely up into the wagon. The team took about two steps and then things really busted loose. The right bay suddenly threw up his head and neighed loudly. Then he plunged forward, smacked into the yoke, and fell back against his startled mate. By this time Mr. T. was scramblin' up the wagon rack, grabbin' for reins and wonderin' wildly if he'd gotten the wrong team.

The bay wasn't finished yet. He began to kick and to buck, strikin' out one way and then the other. By this time he had the other horse convinced that something was seriously wrong and they both decided that they'd best make a run for it. Mr. T. was still scramblin' for his reins when the horses took off on a gallop.

Uncontrolled, they nearly smashed into the wagon of Mr. Corbin but veered at the last minute, comin' very near upsettin' Mr. T's whole wagon. Mr. T. was flailin' his way through bundles tryin' to get hold of the elusive reins. What a ride he had! I think that the team managed to hit every chuck hole and rock in the entire field. Bundles were flyin' out from the wagon on every swerve and bounce. Every man in the field watched the crazy runaway, many of them rushin' to take the reins of their own teams so that they wouldn't get the same notion.

It was Cullum Lewis who finally got things under control. The team was circlin' the field and Cullum watched his chance. When they came near, he made a flyin' leap and grabbed the bridle. Hangin' on for dear life, his feet scrapin' the ground and raisin' a cloud of dust, he pulled on that bridle for all he was worth. To our amazement, the horses came to a stop, heavin' and puffin'. He spent a number of minutes talkin' and strokin' and finally managed to get them quieted again. He calmly handed Mr. T. the limp reins, and still talkin' and pettin' the animals, carefully checked over the harness; he wanted to be sure that in all that buckin' and rearin' nothin' had been broken. A few pieces of harness needed some readjusting to get things back in their proper place. Cullum's hands travelled along each section.

By then I was right there watchin', not wantin' to miss any of the action. Mr. T. was still up on top of what was left of his load, tryin' hard to regain his composure and somehow rationalize in his thinkin' the strange behavior of his bays. He didn't see Cullum lift out a sharp burr from under the right bay's harness, examine it briefly, and then discard it—but I did. Cullum's eyes met mine and he nodded his head jest ever so slightly in the direction of Barkley Shaw. I nodded back. It was our solemn pact to make no mention of the offendin' burr.

"Seems to be okay, Mr. Smith," Cullum called up. "No harness broken, and they seem calm enough now."

Mr. T. jest nodded, his face not seemin' to know if it should be white or red.

He didn't even say thank you, but jest moved the team off, lookin' a bit uncertain at first as to what to expect of them. He had to retrace his trip around the field and pick up the scattered bundles.

I walked along with Cullum toward his waitin' team.

"Want a lift?" he asked.

I nodded.

We climbed up onto the load together and he handed me the reins. We both sat solemnly for a while, and then as if drawn by some outside force, we both turned to each other in the same instant. As soon as our eyes met, we couldn't control ourselves any longer. We laughed all of the way back to the threshin' machine.

Chapter 14

Patches

Monday morning my feet seemed to drag a little; at the same time something within me said "Hurry, hurry." It was the first day back at school. I hated goin' back. The thing that bothered me the most was leaving Gramps. I wasn't sure what he'd find to fill his day with me gone. Of course there was Auntie Lou. Her work would be slowing down now and she would have time for my great-grandfather.

I suppose there were other reasons why I hated to go back. One was the shoes. I had to wear them all day for school and after bein' turned loose all summer, my feet sure did hate to be all shut in. The mornings could be rather cool at times now, and I didn't suppose that I'd fuss much about shoes from now on anyway.

Then there was Auntie Lou. I still missed her when I was away from her, and I had the feeling that with harvest over, Grandpa and Uncle Charlie would take up the "man hunt" again. I didn't like leaving Auntie Lou unguarded.

I suppose the final reason was jest the simple fact that boys are supposed to hate school. School and fancy clothes, sissy games and girls, that's what boys my age didn't go for.

Still, on the other hand, I had to admit that I kinda liked school. It was fun to be with the other boys and play ball or tag or prisoner's base. I didn't have much to play with around the farm.

I would never have admitted it for the world, but I liked the teacher, too. Her name was Martha Peterson. She was the youngest of the Petersons' houseful of girls. She was tall for a woman, but slim as a sapling, and her voice had a soft liltin' sound. I loved to hear her read. During part of each school day she would read us a chapter from a book that she had chosen. We had gone through several books together, and I could never get enough of them.

The truth was I jest plain liked my studies. I know, a boy is supposed to shy away from book learnin'. I didn't. Books held so many interesting facts and figures that I found it awful hard to hide my enthusiasm. Arithmetic was my best subject. I always led the class with no trouble at all, but I also liked spellin' and geography and jest about everything we studied. Didn't care much for the music. Miss Peterson would trill up the scale and we were supposed to follow along behind her. We never could give a decent imitation and it embarrassed and discouraged me. All in all, even though I felt like a traitor to my sex, I liked school.

I think Gramps caught on. His eyes took on a twinkle as if he'd like to scrub up good, slick down his hair, and join me.

It was good to be back. There was a lot of shovin' and yellin' and slappin' one another on the back as we met in the school yard. The bell that I'd been waiting for finally rang and we all trooped noisily in. There was Miss Peterson, smilin' softly, lookin' prettier than ever. I had to keep starin' at my feet to stop the deep red from flushin' up into my face.

The day went quickly and before we knew it we were dismissed. I hated to leave, yet I could hardly wait to get home and tell Gramps and Auntie Lou about my day.

As soon as I got over the rise and out of sight of the school, I whipped off my shoes and stuffed my socks down in the toe of one. I tied the laces together and dangled the shoes over my shoulder jest in case I needed my hands free for throwin' rocks or anything. Then I hitched up my pant legs a couple of rolls to keep them from draggin' in the dust, and set out for home. I ran most of the way. When I finally got in the door I was puffin' so hard that I had to sit down and catch my breath before I could speak. Auntie Lou laughed at my excitement and brought me a big glass of cool milk and some cookies fresh from the oven. Gramps had some too, and finally I was ready to tell about all of my adventures of that first day back at school.

When I had finished eating and talking, I went to change into my chorin' overalls before going out to slop the pigs. Gramps was waiting for me when I came down and we went out together.

"Joshua," he said as we walked along, "I understand that Lou has an eighteenth birthday coming up."

I hadn't thought about it, but now that I did I realized that it was true.

"Yeah—I guess so."

"Anything that you can think of to help make it 'special'?"

I thought for a minute. "She likes parties—but she don't get to go to very many," I finally said.

Gramps thought on it.

"I hardly see how three old men and one young one could come up with much of a party."

"Maybe SueAnn and Nellie Halliday or some of the other girls could help us."

Gramps chewed on his mustache as he thought about that.

"Maybe. Maybe something could be arranged. How could one get in touch with these girls?"

"You could write a note and I'd take it to school and give it to Willie to take home to SueAnn."

"That's good thinking, Joshua."

I beamed at the compliment from Gramps. He abruptly changed the subject.

"Now then we'd best get those chores done."

We finished up the chores. We were even a little ahead of time. The men weren't in from stacking greenfeed yet and supper was not quite ready when I dropped my last load of chopped wood into the wood box. Gramps deposited his load, too, and we stood there brushin' our clothes a bit to get rid of wood chips, grass and bark.

"Got something to show you, Joshua. Come with me."

Gramps led the way to the small shed that stood in the yard. It held our rakes, hoes, wheelbarrow, and such like, so I wasn't sure that I was that much interested in seein' anything in there, but I followed. Maybe Gramps had found a mouse nest or something.

Gramps opened the door; as he did so a funny bit of black and white fur came flyin' at my feet. I jumped like lightnin' had jest warmed my boots, and stepped back a pace. Gramps was chucklin' and scoopin' up the wiggly thing, tryin' to get it under control.

"Didn't expect such an overwhelming welcome," he laughed.

I took a better look then and my breath caught in my throat. It was a pup! I reached my hands out for it, my head full of questions.

"Where'd he come from?"

"From some people in town."

"When?"

"Well, I found him awhile back, but they didn't want me to pick him up until today."

"You were in town today?"

"That's right."

"How?"

"Partly walked, partly hitched a ride."

I blinked in wonder. Gramps had walked and hitched a ride to town! He must have wanted to get there awfully bad.

"Why didn't you ask Grandpa or Uncle Charlie if you needed to get to town that bad?"

"Didn't need to—just wanted to—to pick this fellow up. They didn't get him weaned until last week."

I jerked my attention back to the pup.

"Is he yours?"

Gramps smiled real wide.

"No, Joshua—he's yours."

"Mine?"

My mind couldn't comprehend it, but my arms were already claimin' possession. I pushed my face down against the ball of fur, and had my face licked as a thank you for noticin' him. I laughed and got licked again. I put him down on the ground to get a better look at him. It was hard to do because he wouldn't hold still.

He was still plump with baby fat but looked like he would soon leave that behind and begin to really grow. His hair was mostly black and sort of curly. There were a few white spots here and there and that gave him a comical appearance.

He never was still for a moment, and I could see that he was going to be an awful lot of fun. I scooped him up into my arms again and started lovin' and pettin'.

"My dog! My very own dog!" I kept sayin' over and over to myself, hardly able to believe my good fortune.

Gramps stood by—jest smilin'.

"Hey," I said, "I didn't say 'thanks.'"

"I think you did, Joshua."

"He's beautiful, Gramps, really beautiful. I'm gonna train him to do tricks—sit up, and beg, and play dead, and roll over—and everything!"

"What are you going to call him?"

I thought for a few minutes as I looked at *my* dog. Every name that I ever heard a dog called began to pour through my mind; I rejected each one until I came to Patches. Patches seemed to fit.

"Patches," I said.

"Patches," repeated Gramps. "I think that Patches is a very fitting name."

Gramps chose himself a wood block and turned it up to sit on, so that he could sit and watch me and my dog. I rolled on the grass, he growlin' in a little dog voice and chasin' my pant leg, my sleeve, or even the top of my hair, nippin' and tusslin' and rollin' with me.

We were still playin' our crazy games when Grandpa and Uncle Charlie came home. I hadn't paid much attention until

I was somehow aware that I was being looked at. There stood Grandpa and Uncle Charlie both starin' at me and the dog with puzzled looks on their faces. For one terrifyin' minute I was afraid that they wouldn't let me keep him—my arms automatically tightened on him.

"Where'd—" started Grandpa.

Gramps stood up from the wood block he'd been restin' on; it toppled over as though to take its rightful place back in the pile.

"Got him in town. *Every* boy needs a dog," said Gramps. His keen blue eyes held Grandpa's.

"Reckon so. Shoulda thought myself to get him one—sooner." Grandpa nodded. "Let's see 'im, Boy."

I brought Patches over and introduced him to Grandpa and Uncle Charlie. Grandpa rubbed his head a bit and tugged gently on his ear.

"Looks bright enough."

Then it was Uncle Charlie's turn. He patted the puppy and stroked him under the chin.

"Bet yer gonna be one small piece of nuisance," he said, "but yer bound to liven things up 'round here." His voice held teasin'.

Auntie Lou came out then and I suddenly realized that I had been so preoccupied I hadn't even shown her Patches yet.

"Look!" I cried. "Look what Gramps brought me!"

She smiled and stepped forward to rub the puppy's soft fur with the back of her finger.

"Now, who do you s'pose has been fillin' his tummy with warm milk and holdin' him when he got lonesome for most of the afternoon? But now it's suppertime. How 'bout if you put him back in the shed and come and get washed up."

I did, though it was awfully hard to do.

After supper I took some meat scraps and a saucer of milk to Patches. I begged an old jacket off Uncle Charlie and fixed Patches a comfortable bed in a box low enough for him to come and go as he wanted.

I was called for bed way too soon. It was already 9:00. Reluctantly I left Patches and went in to bed, promisin' him that

I'd be down first thing in the mornin'. I went to bed, my mind boggled with plans for my dog—the doghouse that I'd build, the collar that I'd make him, the tricks that I'd teach him. There was a whole new world waitin' for me now—and all because of Gramps.

I hadn't been talkin' much to God lately. Auntie Lou would have been shocked and hurt had she known.

I was a little hesitant now about prayin' after ignorin' Him for so long, but I finally put aside my pride, crawled out of bed, and got down on my knees.

"Dear God, I wanna say thank you for a few things. I know sometimes I don't think you're doin' much special-like for me, but I do wanna thank you for bringin' Gramps here—even iffen I didn't want him at first. I really love him now, God. And thank you for Patches, too. Help me to make him a good dog so that he won't be *too* much of a nuisance. Amen."

I climbed back into bed and pulled the quilt up to my chin. I went to sleep with my mind full of pictures of me and my dog.

Chapter 15

Hurtin'

The next mornin' I was nearly torn in two with desire. I wanted to get to school as fast as I could to tell all of the boys about my new dog. At the same time I didn't want to leave him. If only I could have gathered him up and taken him to school with me—but even I understood that that was out of the question.

I finally tore myself away from him at the last possible minute, promising that I'd be home again jest as quickly as I could. I asked Gramps if he'd let Patches out of the shed as soon as I'd gone and he couldn't follow, so that he could get acquainted with the farm and not be locked up and bored all day.

I got to school, puffin' and pantin' because I had run so hard; before the bell rang I was only able to blurt out that I had a new dog. The boys were full of questions and I answered as many as I could while we hurried to line up for salutin' the flag and prayin' the Lord's Prayer. Avery and Willie promised to come over to see Patches the first chance that they got.

At recess and noon break we talked about my dog. I described him over and over, and some of the boys got almost as excited as I was. The news even got to the girls, and Sarah Smith and Mary Turley worked up enough nerve to come over to the boys' side to question me about him. I really felt important.

Miss Peterson had scarcely said "Class dismissed" when I was gone. I had so much to do. I didn't know whether to start on the collar and lead rope first, or work on the doghouse. Patches needed both.

I was callin' him as I ran down the lane, but I didn't notice him around anywhere.

Auntie Lou came out.

"Josh, come in the house a minute—will you?"

"Sure," I called back. "Soon's I find Patches."

"Right *now*, Josh."

I went. Maybe they had Patches with them.

A glass of milk and a piece of cake sat at my place at the table. Gramps sat there, too, but he wasn't havin' anything. Auntie Lou looked rather pale and her eyes looked suspiciously like she'd been cryin'. My mind jumped to Grandpa and Uncle Charlie, and I felt a scare hit me smack in my stomach.

"Sit down, Josh."

I sat. I jest sat like a lump and stared first at Auntie Lou and then at Gramps.

Auntie Lou swallowed hard and she bit her lip to fight back tears. Finally she was able to talk, in a soft quivery voice.

"A bad thing happened today, Josh."

I knew that much. I could tell by jest lookin'.

"Your puppy was killed."

I fought it. I fought it with all my strength. It couldn't be true, it jest couldn't. But a look at Gramps' white face and a quick glance at Auntie Lou, who was liftin' a damp handkerchief to her eyes, told me that I had to believe it.

I didn't wait to even say anything. I jest jumped up from the table, spillin' my milk, and ran for the door.

"Josh!" I heard Auntie Lou's voice.

"Let him go," said Gramps softly. His voice sounded old and tired.

I ran all the way to the crik. I wished that I could jest throw myself right into the cold water and let it wash all the feelin' from me. I threw myself on the grassy bank instead. Boys weren't supposed to cry—but I cried. I cried until my eyes ran dry, and then I jest laid and groaned.

It was gettin' dark when I finally lifted myself from the bank. It was gettin' cold, too. I hadn't noticed before, but now I realized that I was shiverin'. I knelt down by the stream and sloshed cold water over my face again and again. It nearly froze me but it sharpened things back into focus, too. Here it was dark and I hadn't done one bit of my chores. Grandpa and Uncle Charlie would be in from stackin' the greenfeed and I wouldn't have my work done. I started home at a trot.

As my mind began to clear, I found myself wonderin' how it had happened. What had gone wrong? The pup I had wanted for so long had been mine for such a short time— hardly long enough to even get the feel that he *was* mine.

When I got to the house, I found that Gramps had done all of my chores. It had taken him longer than it took me. It was a big and difficult job for an old man like Gramps. Auntie Lou had milked Bossie and helped to split the wood. It made me feel shame—but a great deal of love and gratitude, too. I wanted to start cryin' all over again, but I held myself in check.

Uncle Charlie and Grandpa had returned and supper had been served. Auntie Lou had a plateful of food saved for me in the warmin' oven. I tried to eat it but it was tough to get it past the lump in my throat.

For the first time in my life I didn't wait for Grandpa to say, "Bedtime, Boy"; I went up on my own, glad to get to my room and shut the door.

I wouldn't cry anymore. I was through with that now. I laid there quietly and let anger and disappointment seep from every pore. Why? Why? Why?

Gramps came up. He opened my door softly and hesitated at my door.

"Joshua?"

I couldn't say "go away"—not to Gramps.

"Yeah."

"Do you mind?"

"It's okay."

He came forward and sat on my bed. He sat there quietly for a while and then reached out an old hand that was soft, not calloused and rough from work like Grandpa's or Uncle Charlie's, though I knew that for most of his life it had been. He touched my arm.

"I know how you hurt, Joshua."

I didn't even think, "No you don't, no you don't." Somehow I knew that he did.

"It's not easy to lose someone you love."

I gulped. If he wasn't careful I'd be cryin' again.

"I thought that you might like to know what happened."

I waited. I did want to know and I didn't.

"Patches was a busy little dog—and a smart one. But I guess he just figured that he knew a little more than he really did."

I waited.

"The range cattle were pasturing just across the fence from the garden, and I guess Patches decided that he'd be a cattle dog. Anyway, Lou and I heard the ruckus, but by the time that we got there he'd been kicked. We tried to save him but—"

He stopped there. In my mind I could see Auntie Lou with tears runnin' down her face, and my grey-haired Gramps workin' over the broken body of my little dog. Tears came again and I swallowed them away.

Gramps patted me gently, got up and moved toward the door. I was glad that he hadn't expected me to talk. I couldn't talk now.

I laid there thinkin' about my little dog, and then a lot of other bitter thoughts started comin' to me, too. I used them like a blanket, wrappin' myself up in them and findin' a queer kind of satisfaction in the thought that I had suffered more than anyone else in the world. Bitterness filled me until I could hold no more. I sniffed.

My door opened again. Auntie Lou slipped in.

"Don't cry, Josh," she pleaded, soundin' like she needed the admonition more than I did.

"I ain't cryin'."

Now Auntie Lou could hear a sniff behind a three-foot

solid rock wall, but she didn't argue with me; she jest sat beside me much as Gramps had done.

"I'm sorry, Josh—so sorry."

I knew that she was.

"There was jest no way that we could have stopped it."

"God could've."

There, it was out now—in two angry, accusin' words.

Auntie Lou sorta caught her breath, but I didn't wait for her to say anything.

"I even prayed last night, and I thanked Him for Gramps and I thanked Him for Patches, and then without even waitin' He lets my dog die. He could have stopped it! He could have! He doesn't care, that's what. He jest hurts and hurts, and iffen He thinks that I'm gonna love Him—I'm not—I won't."

I was sobbin' now and Auntie Lou sat quietly as though my words had completely stunned her.

I flipped over on my stomach.

"He doesn't even leave me memories," I almost shouted. "He takes everything."

Auntie Lou let me cry until I had completely drained myself of tears. When I finally lay quietly she took my hand and stroked it gently, feelin' each of my fingers separately.

"Josh?"

I managed to say, "Yeah."

"What did you mean about memories—about not havin' any?"

I swallowed once or twice.

"It was the same with my ma and pa," I muttered. "God took 'em, too, before I could have any memories. Grandpa has memories. Lots of them. He told me all about Grandma and Great-grandma, too. And Gramps told me all about the good years when Great-grandma was still with him. Uncle Charlie remembers, too, but *I* don't remember *nothin'*—*not one thing*."

I started to whimper again.

"Josh."

"What?"

"Josh, I don't remember *my* ma either, but I have *lots* of memories."

I looked at her in the pale light, wonderin' if she'd lost her senses.

"My mama died before I was old enough to remember her. I know that she loved me—I jest feel it; but I don't remember one thing about her, not one."

"Then how—"

"My memories are different, but they're jest as real and jest as filled with love.

"I remember Pa's face above my crib, his eyes laughin' as he played with me. I remember Uncle Charlie givin' me a ride on his foot and sayin', 'This is the way the lady rides.' I remember Pa rockin' me and holdin' me before he tucked me into bed at night. I remember him leanin' over me, his hand on my cheek, a worried look in his eyes when I had the measles, and I remember them both stayin' beside my bed all night long one winter when I had the croup. They took turns for four days—day and night.

"Josh, I remember a tiny baby that was brought home wrapped in blankets, and when I asked Pa why, he swallowed away tears and said that the baby was mine to care for now. He needed me. I remember dressin' him and feedin' him and playin' with him—and lovin' him."

There was a pause while Auntie Lou struggled for control.

"I have lots of memories, Josh—lots of *good* memories."

It was little more than a whisper.

As I listened to Auntie Lou talk, I realized that I had some memories, too. I'd jest been lookin' in the wrong place for them. Like families, memories didn't come in only one kind of package.

I was fightin' an inward battle now. I was still angry and wantin' to strike back.

"He still didn't need to take my dog."

"Josh, God *didn't* take your dog. It was jest—jest one of those things that happens, that's all."

"But He coulda *stopped* it."

Auntie Lou hesitated a moment as she carefully thought through her next words.

"Yes, He could have. He could let us go through all of our life, bundlin' us and shelterin' us from anything and everything that would hurt us. I could do that with my petunias,

Josh. I could build a box around them and keep them from the wind and the rain, the crawlers and the bees. What would happen iffen I did that, Josh?"

I jest shrugged. The answer was too obvious.

"They'd never bear flowers," said Auntie Lou.

"Josh, I don't understand all about God, but there's one thing that I'm as sure of as the fact that I live and breathe. He loves us. He loves us completely, and always keeps our good in mind.

"I don't know how losin' your pup is for your good, Josh, but I *am* sure that it *can* be or God wouldn't have let it happen. It's all up to you, Josh. Whenever something comes into our life that hurts us, we do the decidin'—do I let this work for my good, as God intended, or do I let bitterness grow like a bothersome canker sore in my soul?

"We love you, Josh—every one of us. We don't want to see you hurt. It's happened now. We can't change it, but don't give the hurt a chance to grow even bigger and destroy you. God *loves* you. He can help you with the hurt if you ask Him to; accept that even *this* can be for your good. Try, Josh. Please try."

Auntie Lou bent down and kissed me. Her cheeks were wet as they touched mine. She left the room.

I laid there thinkin' of all that she'd said. I decided that one day soon, maybe down by the crik, I'd work on some memories and see jest what I could come up with. Even as I laid there I saw a blue-eyed, laughin' pixie face bendin' over me, cooin' love words—my Auntie Lou. I pushed it aside. I didn't want to get love feelin's all mixed in with my bitter ones. The one might somehow destroy the other.

Auntie Lou loved me, of that I had no question. So did Gramps, and even, I was willin' to admit, Grandpa and Uncle Charlie. But God? Somehow that jest didn't add up.

If He did love me He sure chose some strange ways of showin' it. I knew that Auntie Lou wouldn't want me to hate God. I was even a little afraid of the consequences myself. No, I decided, I wouldn't hate Him—but I couldn't love Him either. I'd jest feel nothin'—nothin' at all. I wouldn't even think about Him. I'd jest ignore Him completely. That would give Him something to think about. Maybe He'd even feel sorry.

Chapter 16

Love in Action

I dreaded having to go back to school. I'd have to tell all the kids about my pup. I hated it. If ever I'd been tempted to play hooky, that was the day. I considered takin' my lunch pail and jest headin' for the crik, but I realized that I would then be cornered into tellin' lies to Auntie Lou; I jest couldn't stand the thought of that. I dragged to school, faced my friends with the facts, and dragged home again.

When I entered the kitchen, Auntie Lou was fussin' over Gramps.

"Please," she was saying, "drink up your tea. You look all done in."

My eyes turned to Gramps. He did look awfully tired. I hoped that he wasn't gettin' sick or something.

I said between clenched teeth, "If *you* take him, too. . ." My hands were at my sides tightenin' into fists.

Gramps smiled at me, rather weakly, but he showed spunk.

"Howdy, Joshua."

"Howdy."

I slipped into my chair jest as Auntie Lou set my juice down.

"Hurry with your juice, Josh. Gramps has something to show you."

After my juice was gulped down, Gramps led me to the shed again. Inside was a carefully made little box. The lid was already down. I guessed that Gramps thought it best that I not see Patches' trampled body. There was a marker there, too. It was a long sharp-pointed stick with another stick across the top of it on which were painted the words, "Patches—Joshua's first dog."

"I thought that maybe *you'd* like to—"

"Where?" I asked as I swallowed hard and nodded.

I led the way, carryin' the box. Gramps followed with a shovel. There was a bit of soft soil under the big maple tree at the end of Auntie Lou's garden. When I reached the tree I put the box down and took the shovel from Gramps.

We said nothin' until the box was lowered and covered and the marker pounded in the ground. "Patches—Joshua's first dog." I wondered at Gramps' choice of words. Auntie Lou came and put a little bouquet of late fall flowers on the tiny grave.

"In the spring," she said, "we'll plant a violet."

I looked at the two of them.

"Thanks," I said, and picked up the shovel and started off to get ready for chores.

"Joshua," called Gramps. "There's just one more thing."

Surely he wasn't askin' me to pray over that dead dog. I stopped.

"In the house," prompted Gramps.

I walked obediently into the kitchen and jest stood waitin'.

Gramps shuffled past me. He did seem tired. I'd never seen him walk like that before—without a spring to his step.

In a minute he was back from his room with something concealed beneath his sweater. When he reached in, there was a bit of motion to the lump and then a soft nose peaked out, followed by two bright, almost black eyes.

"I know that she isn't Patches," said Gramps, untanglin'

her feet from his sweater, "but she could be a lot of fun."

He handed her to me. She was so little. Only a baby, really. Her hair was soft brown curls, her little ears drooped over her fine shaped head and her tail was curled and fluffy.

"She's pretty young to leave her mother," said Gramps, "so we'll have to be extra careful with her. She's going to be awfully lonesome for a while, Joshua. She'll need lots of love."

I jest held her, marvellin' that a puppy could be so tiny and so perfect. Her little tongue licked against my hand. She knew that much already.

"She'll never be a cattle dog," continued Gramps, "never be big enough for that. She won't be very big at all. I couldn't find—"

"She's fine," I cut in. I got the impression that Gramps was apologizin' about the puppy. "She's beautiful. Jest look—jest look at her face. Bet she'll learn tricks fast. Bet she might even learn how to walk on her hind legs and dance."

That *something* that had seemed dead within me was stirrin' to life again. I felt excitement creepin' through me.

I heard a sigh of relief escape Auntie Lou, and Gramps' face looked less tired.

I hugged the puppy again. She was small enough that I could hold her firmly in my two hands.

"What you gonna call her?" asked Auntie Lou.

"I don't know. I'll have to think on it while I'm chorin'. Boy—I gotta get chorin', too!"

I pulled myself away from fondlin' my puppy.

"Gramps, would you mind sorta watchin' her while I do the chores?"

Gramps grinned.

"She does look a little sleepy, doesn't she? Maybe I'll just take her in on my bed so that she can catch a little nap."

I handed the puppy to Gramps and watched as he walked to his room, talkin' softly to her.

"Thanks, Josh," whispered Auntie Lou. "He is so tired—I've been worried. I was afraid that if he went chorin' with you tonight, it would be jest too much for him."

"Is he sick?" I asked anxiously.

"No, jest tired." Auntie Lou shook her head.

"As soon as you left for school this mornin' Josh, Gramps left for town to find you another pup. I don't know how far he walked before gettin' a ride. When he got to town he walked the streets lookin' for a dog with pups. This was the only litter he found and they were really too young to wean, but Mrs. Sankey, the owner, finally let Gramps take his pick from the lot. He tried 'em, one by one, to see if he could find one that would drink from a saucer. This was the smallest one of the bunch, but she caught on quickly 'bout how to lap up milk. Gramps walked home carryin' her. She's pretty special, Josh."

I nodded. She was special all right. Seemed like she should be called "Miracle" or "Love-gift" or something like that.

I sneaked to Gramps' door. I wanted to tell him thank-you if I could get it past the lump in my throat.

He was already sleepin'—snorin' softly. The puppy was cuddled up in his arms against his chest. I swallowed again. I'd have to tell him later, and it was sure gonna be hard to put my feelings into fittin' words.

Chapter 17

Pixie

I called the puppy Pixie. The name suited her. She was a tiny, playful and mischievous bit of fur, and we all took to her right away. I didn't bother to build her a doghouse. Everyone liked her so much that it was jest an accepted fact that a little mite like her couldn't sleep out of doors. Maybe it was because Grandpa and Uncle Charlie had a soft spot for raisin' babies. At any rate we fixed a box for Pixie near the kitchen stove where she could snuggle down in Gramps' old gray sweater during the day.

At night I took her up to bed with me and no one protested. I wasn't sure if it was for my comfortin' or that of the dog's, that they let me get away with it—but they did.

She was smart all right and from the start she entertained us. My whole world about turned around her, and I had to really take myself in hand to get my thoughts on other things.

Gramps reminded me again of Auntie Lou's comin' birthday, and together one night we composed a letter for SueAnn. I carefully tucked it into my pocket; I'd deliver it to Willie the next day.

SueAnn wasn't long in replying. She and some of the other girls would be more than happy to help with a party. She suggested a corn roast and said that the girls would be glad to care for the lunch. If Gramps could see that there was wood for the fire, they'd do the rest.

Gramps was pleased with the letter. He sat down right away and wrote to her again, confirming the plans and setting the date. He pulled a bill from a small box in his dresser drawer and tucked it in with the letter; the money would help the girls with their expenses for the refreshments. I took that letter to Willie, too, and he took it home to SueAnn.

Uncle Charlie and Grandpa finished the stackin' of the greenfeed and the good fall weather still held.

I had only a few chores that were my responsibility now. Uncle Charlie took over most of them again, and Auntie Lou took back the carin' for her chickens.

The last vegetables of the garden were dug and were carefully stored in the root cellar. Odd jobs for the final preparations for winter were finished. It about got to the place that it wouldn't have mattered none if a storm had decided to strike—even though we'd take all of the fair weather that we could get—but none did.

The only thing that we really were concerned about was Auntie Lou's coming party. If we could jest hold onto the good weather until after that, then we'd take whatever the season decided to send our way.

We men managed to find some talkin' time as we finished up the chores one night. Gramps had clued in Grandpa and Uncle Charlie about the plans for the party before we had written SueAnn. They were pleased about it and anxious to be a part of the action.

The party was set for a Saturday night—Lou's birthday. We decided to work in a trip to town as early as we could get away Saturday mornin'. Then we could give Auntie Lou her gifts and have our own little celebration at supper—and maybe throw her off the scent.

I gathered the coins that I had managed to collect. They didn't make much of a pile. I finally got up the nerve to ask

Gramps if he'd mind if I threw in the two dimes, seein' that we wouldn't be doin' anymore fishin' before winter, anyway. He said that that would be fine and I felt a little better.

When we got to the store, we did an awful lot of lookin' before we made up our minds.

Uncle Charlie finally settled on a shawl. It was a lacy-lookin' thing. Didn't look much for warmth but it sure was pretty.

Grandpa chose a new dress. It was cream colored with pink ribbons here and there and lots of lace for trimmin'. I could jest imagine what Auntie Lou would look like in it.

I found a lace handkerchief that really drew my eye, but when I counted my money, I didn't have enough. I kept on lookin'. I never did spot anything else as pretty as the handkerchief, and I was still lookin' when the rest were ready to go.

Uncle Charlie saw me eyein' the hanky, and I guess he figured out real quick what the problem was. I felt him slip some coins into my pocket. With mine, it paid for the handkerchief and left a nickel over. I studied the candy as Mrs. Kirk wrapped up the handkerchief, but then I turned away from it, determined to give Uncle Charlie back his nickel.

We met Gramps outside at the wagon. He'd been down the street to another store and made his purchase there. On the way home he showed it to me.

"It sure is pretty all right," I agreed. "What's it for?"

"It's a box to keep jewelry in."

I didn't know whether to tell him or jest let it pass. Finally I said it.

"Looks like a first-rate jew'ry box, Gramps, but there's only one problem."

Gramps looked up at me funny-like.

"She don't got none," I whispered.

Gramps jest shook his head and smiled.

"But she *will* have," he said. "She will have."

Maybe that *was* the smart way to go, I decided. You get the box first and *then* you get the jew'ry.

We could hardly wait to finish the chores. Even Pixie took second place to Auntie Lou's birthday.

Lou knew that she was expected to have a cake ready for herself. She had been bakin' the birthday cakes in this house ever since she was big enough to use the oven. She had her cake ready and sittin' in the middle of the table. We all grinned at it and could hardly wait to get the meal over with.

We gave Auntie Lou our gifts jest before she cut the cake. They let me be first. I presented her with the handkerchief.

"Oh, Josh," she cried, "it's jest beautiful! Where'd you ever get enough money to buy such a pretty one?"

I looked at Uncle Charlie. He stared at me blankly like he didn't know a thing about it. Auntie Lou gave me a warm hug.

She opened Uncle Charlie's shawl next and that really set her eyes to sparklin'. Uncle Charlie got a hug, too, which he seemed mighty pleased about.

Grandpa handed Lou his gift. She lifted the beautiful cream and pink dress from the box and shook out the folds.

"Oh, Pa, it's beautiful. Really beautiful. I know that I don't really need it, but—but I'm glad that you bought it. It's so pretty."

That was Lou. None of this I-wish-you-hadn't-done-it stuff. She said jest what she really felt.

"I'll feel so dressed up—so special. I hope that something important happens real soon to give me a chance to wear it all."

"Go put it on," coaxed Gramps.

"Should I?" Lou's cheeks were flushed.

We all urged her to try on the finery. We were all anxious to see jest how good our purchases could look.

Lou laughed and gathered up her gifts. She was soon back whirlin' her skirts and laughin' as she pranced around the kitchen.

The dress fit her perfectly. The cream color enhanced the creaminess of her skin and the pink bows seemed about to match her cheeks.

She draped the shawl about her shoulders, waved her lace handkerchief and pretended to flirt. We all laughed.

We were enjoyin' it so that at first I didn't notice Gramps stand up. He cleared his throat and then stepped forward.

"I have something for you, too, Louisa."

Lou stopped flutterin'. Gramps handed her his package. Lou opened it carefully and gave a little gasp when she saw the embossed box.

"A jewelry box!"

I was relieved that she hadn't had to ask what the thing was.

"It's lovely, Gramps."

"Open it, Louisa."

She did, and there on the soft velvet lay the most beautiful locket that I had ever seen. It hadn't been there before when Gramps had showed me the box, I was sure of that.

Auntie Lou's big blue eyes got even bigger. She couldn't even speak. She looked down at the locket, then she gently lifted it out and let it lay in her hand.

"It was your grandmother's," Gramps said in a hushed voice. "It can be worn only by the world's most beautiful and sweetest women—your grandmother and you."

Gramps moved forward and took the locket from Auntie Lou. He stepped behind her and fastened the chain around her slim neck. Then he kissed her on the cheek.

"Happy eighteenth, Louisa."

Lou was cryin' by then, and she made the rounds again, kissin' and huggin' each one of "her men."

We probably would have kept right on laughin' and lovin' all night if Uncle Charlie hadn't suddenly noticed the clock. He drew our attention to it with a nod of his head.

Grandpa suggested the cake then. Lou made her wish and blew out the candles. Then she served us each a generous piece. She ate a small piece herself and then ran laughin' to change back into her workin' clothes.

I shared my piece with Pixie. I didn't dare give her too much for fear that it would upset her little tummy. She loved it. She licked her chops with her tiny pink tongue and then licked off my fingers to make sure that she got everythng that was available to her.

We all sat talkin', the men drinkin' coffee and me washin' down my cake with milk. It had been a pretty good birthday party. We couldn't see how the next half of it could be any better. Still, we were pleased that it was still to come.

Out of the blue Grandpa sorta spoiled it for me. He turned to Uncle Charlie.

"Burt Thomas will be comin'?"

Uncle Charlie jest nodded.

So that was the next name on the list. I gathered up Pixie and started outside thinkin', *Why spoil everything? We have Auntie Lou, She's happy here. Didn't you see her laughin'? Why spoil it?*

Chapter 18

The Corn Roast

It was almost eight o'clock before the teams started pourin' in. Auntie Lou looked out of the window wonderin' what in the world was goin' on. It took her awhile to realize that it might have something to do with her.

I figured that everybody in the whole countryside, between the ages of seventeen and thirty, must be pullin' into our yard. There were even a few that I couldn't put a name to.

SueAnn Corbin and Rachael Morgan came in laughin' to drag Auntie Lou out. She begged time to change her dress first and it was granted. I wondered about the new cream birthday dress, but Auntie Lou had more sense than to put that on. She dressed instead in a wide-skirted cotton print with white collar and cuffs. She looked great, but then she always did.

While the girls were gettin' things set up on an outside table that Grandpa had put there for their use, the boys took care of the teams. Our barnyard was full of feedin' horses, unhitched from their wagons and tethered to the rail fences.

It was noisy out in the yard. It seemed to me that no one really talked. The boys all yelled and the girls jest giggled.

After things sorta settled down, SueAnn started some outdoor games. I found a spot beside the honeysuckle bush where I could watch the goings-on without bein' in anyone's way. I sat there, cuddlin' Pixie and wonderin' what it would be like to be part of the action. Everytime a girl squealed or giggled real loudly, I was glad that I had no part of it. The fellas didn't seem to mind though; in fact, I kind of got the idea that they deliberately did things that would make the girls squeal even louder.

The first game was one in which you needed partners. Auntie Lou was paired up with "Toad" Hopkins. He looked awfully pleased with himself. The game was a funny kind of a relay in which Lou and Toad almost won, but Burt Thomas and Nellie Halliday managed to beat them.

Several other games were played. It seemed to me that each one got a little louder and a little faster. Anyway, they sure seemed to be havin' a good time.

I noticed Cullum Lewis. He wasn't as rowdy as some of them, but he did look to be enjoyin' himself. Poor Cullum. I didn't suppose that he got to have a good time very often. His pa had been sick most of the time when Cullum was growin' up. There were seven kids in the family and five of them were girls. Cullum was the only boy for most of the time, and then the final baby turned out to be a boy, too. He was still only about four and spoiled rotten.

Cullum had to take over the farm when he was jest a kid, quittin' school early. At first the farm didn't do much; anyway, everything that Cullum was able to scrape together had to go to pay off his pa's debts. I didn't s'pose he was totally clear of the debts yet, but as hard as he worked, I hoped that the day would soon come when he would be. He still had his ma, five sisters, and a kid brother to care for. With all of that restin' on his young shoulders, no wonder he was more serious than the other young bucks his age. Now as I watched him, he joined in the games with the others but not with the same silliness. One thing I did notice though—he sure kept close track of Auntie Lou. His eyes followed her wherever she went with kind of a haunted, hungry look.

My teacher, Miss Martha Peterson, was at the party, too. Funny, I hadn't thought of her as a young person before, but I guess she was only three or four years older than Auntie Lou. Some folks said that Barkley Shaw was sweet on her, but from what I saw, Barkley Shaw was sweet on anything in a skirt. I didn't care much for Barkley.

Grandpa stood beside me for a while watchin' the action. I could see him smile every now and then as though he heartily approved.

"Lou seems to be havin' fun, don't she?"

"Guess so."

Grandpa stood a minute deep in thought.

"She oughta have fun more often."

He pulled his watch out and checked the time. I could tell by the look on his face that it must be nine o'clock. I expected him to say, "Bedtime, Boy," but he didn't. Instead he said, "Tonight's a little special"; then tucked the watch away. I knew that was my permission to stay up.

The games ended and the open fire was lit. People carried blocks from the woodpile and placed them around in a circle, side by side, with the fire in the middle. Amid much banter and teasin' the corn roastin' began. The other food was laid out, too, and it looked like they would have quite a feast.

Grandpa appeared again.

"Lou," he called, nice and loud, "yer Uncle Charlie made a big pot of hot chocolate and it's ready. Burt, would you mind givin' Lou a hand?"

So there it was, I thought. I'd wondered how and when they'd weasel him in.

Burt walked off with Lou, grinnin' rather foolishly. Barkley looked a little annoyed. He had placed his block right next to Auntie Lou's at the fire and had busied himself with explainin' to her the best way to roast a cob—or something.

Barkley was older than the other guys, but that sure didn't make him any less a kid. After Lou had left, Barkley shrugged and busied himself with smearin' butter on the block that Burt had jest been sittin' on, tellin' everyone in a loud voice to "jest you watch when the dummy gets back."

Barkley had his back turned and was loudly teasin' Nellie

and SueAnn when one of the fellows switched the woodblocks. When Barkley took his seat again, he found that *he* was sittin' in the butter. I don't think that Barkley ever did know who did it, but I did. It was done jest as quietly and seriously as Cullum did everything that he did. No one else had even noticed him.

It seemed to take Auntie Lou and Burt an awful long time to get out there with that hot chocolate. I wondered jest what kind of a trick Uncle Charlie and Grandpa were usin' to detain them. Eventually they returned, and Burt seemed to assume that he now had earned his place beside Auntie Lou for the rest of the evenin'.

I was sittin' there studying all the commotion when there was a quiet voice beside me.

"Brought ya some grub, Josh."

I jumped so that I woke up Pixie who was asleep on my lap. I was so sure that no one could see me there where I was sittin'.

It was Cullum.

"Thought thet yer stomach must be fair growlin' eyein' all thet food an' not gittin' any."

"Thanks," I said, takin' it. I *was* powerful hungry.

"Got ya a dog, huh?"

Cullum reached down and picked up Pixie in his big man hands. He stroked her hair gently and chuckled to himself. I knew that he liked her. He didn't even have to say so.

"Can I git ya some more?"

"That's lots—thanks, Cullum. Me, I gotta go to bed soon anyway."

Cullum laid Pixie back on my lap and stood up.

"Good party," he said. He was lookin' at Auntie Lou.

"Yeah," I answered. I don't know why but I got the feelin' that Cullum might kinda like to talk about Lou for a while.

"We kinda had our own party before this one."

"Ya did?"

"Yeah. We gave her our presents at supper time."

"What'd *you* give her?"

"A hanky—handkerchief," I corrected, "all lace and stuff."

"Bet she liked it."

"Yeah, she did. Said it was the prettiest she'd ever seen. And Uncle Charlie gave her a new shawl. She'll prob'ly wear it to church—maybe tomorrow. Maybe you'll—"

I caught myself too late. None of the Lewises ever went to church. I hurried on.

"An' Grandpa gave her a new dress. Boy, is it pretty. Looks real nice on her, too. She tried it on already. She hopes that somebody gets married soon or somethin' so that she can wear it."

Cullum was still watchin' Auntie Lou.

"And Gramps gave her a jew'ry box and a locket on a little chain that used to be my great-grandmother's."

Burt Thomas was sayin' something to Auntie Lou and makin' her laugh. Cullum shifted his feet.

"Guess I'd better be headin' home, Josh. Got a little further to go than some of 'em."

He moved as though he was leavin'. I jumped up, almost forgettin' to rescue Pixie from bein' dumped on the ground.

"Jest wait a minute, okay?" I said hurriedly and shoved Pixie at him. "Here, hold her a minute."

It was hard to get close enough to tug on Auntie Lou's skirt. I jest waved my head and she excused herself and followed me. I could see her eyes askin' me if something was wrong, so as quickly as possible I blurted out my reason.

"Cullum has to go home early. He has a long way to drive. I jest thought that you'd like to thank him for comin', that's all."

Her face relaxed then and she put her hand on my shoulder and we walked over to Cullum. He was standin' there strokin' Pixie. He was such a big man, holdin' such a little dog, that it looked rather comical.

"Josh tells me that you need to leave," said Auntie Lou in a soft voice.

"Thet's right," answered Cullum, still fondlin' Pixie. "Takes awhile to make the drive an' I need to be up early in the mornin'. Not through with my own fall work yet, havin' worked the threshin' crew fer so long."

Auntie Lou nodded and I could guess that she was thinkin', *Tomorrow is the Lord's day*, but she didn't say so. She gave Cullum a warm smile and extended her hand. Cullum nearly dropped Pixie and I reached out to save her from impendin' disaster.

"Thank you so much for comin', Cullum. I know that you're very busy, and I do appreciate your helpin' me to celebrate my birthday."

Auntie Lou spoke the words sincerely, and I knew that she meant every one of them.

"My pleasure," replied Cullum, and I knew that he meant that, too.

Auntie Lou retrieved her hand.

"I hope that you get your harvest all cared for before a storm."

He nodded. "Thank ya."

Someone by the fire called for Auntie Lou. *If it's Burt Thomas*, I thought, *I'll wring his neck*. Auntie Lou looked around.

"I must go," she apologized. "Thank you again, Cullum."

"I was wonderin'—"

But she had turned and was leavin' and she didn't look back. I was sure that she hadn't caught the softly spoken words of Cullum. I moved forward to run after her but Cullum's hand stopped me.

"Take good care of thet pup, Josh." Then he was gone.

I went into the house then. I'd had enough. Burt Thomas was still hangin' 'round Auntie Lou like a fly around molasses, and Barkley Shaw was still teasin' all of the girls and showin' off in spite of the melted butter on the seat of his pants.

I felt a little upset with Auntie Lou. She could have been nicer to Cullum—jest given him an extra smile, or a flutter of the eyelashes, or one of those tricks that girls use—but Auntie Lou never did those things. Maybe she *did* like Cullum. I didn't know, but I sure could guess how Cullum felt about her. I felt sorry for Cullum. I would fight with every inch of me to keep Auntie Lou, but if the day ever did come when I had to lose her, I sure was cheerin' for Cullum.

I ran to shut the chicken-house door that I had forgotten in all of the excitement, and then I went into the house. It was chilly outside by now and in the kitchen I leaned close to the stove to soak up a little warmth before goin' up to bed.

Auntie Lou came in. She was alone.

"Like a piece of cake, Josh?"

I didn't answer. I was still put out with her, and I wanted to be sure that she'd get the message.

"Cake, Josh?" she said again.

When I still didn't answer she came over to me.

"Something wrong?" Her eyes checked Pixie to make sure that the dog was okay.

"Pa send ya to bed?" she tried again.

"Nope."

"Then what—"

"I jest figure that ya coulda been a little nicer, that's all. Here he comes all the way over here and all, and. . ." I really didn't know what to accuse Auntie Lou of.

"I thanked him for comin'—and I meant it, Josh."

"Yeah, but ya didn't thank him very good," I blurted. "Ya coulda—ya coulda giggled or something."

Auntie Lou looked at me sharply. I think that she understood it all then.

"Josh," she said. "I like Cullum, truly I do—as a man, as a friend; but, Josh," she searched for words, "Cullum has never—has never had time for God. I don't know that—that he even believes that there *is* a God.

"I'm happy, Josh, to have Cullum call, to be neighborly, to—uh—speak with and all. I like him. He's a nice man; but, Josh, I could never like Cullum in any other way—not as long as he chooses to leave God out of his life."

"I didn't say ya had to marry him," I snapped; "jest sort of make him—make him feel good by bein' extra nice."

"Joshua!"

Auntie Lou hardly ever called me by my full name.

"Cullum is too fine a man to play games with. I wouldn't mislead or hurt him for the world. I could never encourage him, and it wouldn't be fair to pretend that I could."

She was right, of course. I knew that. I was glad to hear that Auntie Lou thought that Cullum was a fine man. Maybe if he knew, he'd start goin' to church, and then Auntie Lou would feel different about it. But even as the thought came to me, I knew that it would take more than just his *showin'* at church. Auntie Lou would want to be good and sure that he felt about God like she did before she committed herself in any way.

Auntie Lou suddenly realized that she should be outside. They were busy cleanin' up now. They'd all soon be goin' home. She wrapped her shawl tightly about her shoulders and went out.

"Good-night, Josh."

"Good-night."

I turned to go up to bed and then decided to get a little more warmth first. I sat down on the kitchen floor, curled up tightly against the wall and close to the big old stove. I got drowsy sittin' there in the warmth. Pixie was sound asleep in my arms. I knew that I should move to my bed before I did fall asleep, but it was so warm and comfortable there. Uncle Charlie and Grandpa were both helpin' with the clean-up and Gramps had long ago taken to his bed.

I tried rousin' myself again and then I heard voices. It was Auntie Lou and dumb ol' Burt Thomas. I supposed that Grandpa and Uncle Charlie had sent them in again. Burt was sayin' something to Auntie Lou.

"Is that so?" she said, but she didn't sound very excited about it.

"I've always thought so, an' now tonight I realize it even more."

Auntie Lou didn't respond—jest started pilin' dirty dishes on the kitchen table.

"Really, Lou," Burt continued, and he sounded like he was in pain or something. "I care about ya an awful lot. You're the only girl thet I've ever felt this way about."

Lou was probably thinkin' right then about Tillie Whitecomb, who'd been Burt's girl last month, or Marjorie Anderson, who had been the one the month before.

"Oh," she said—not even a "thank ya for the compliment" or "you flatter me," or nothin'."

Burt suddenly seemed to feel that talkin' was gettin' him

nowhere, and before Auntie Lou could even move he whirled her about, jerked her close and kissed her.

Everything stopped. I expected thunder and lightnin'. Auntie Lou pushed herself away from Burt and back a pace. Her eyes flashed. I was hopin' that she would hit him, but she didn't. She jest stood there with her eyes blazin', and when she spoke her voice was even and cold.

"Burt Thomas, don't you ever come near me again!" She spun on her heel, her skirts swishin' angrily, and was gone.

No one had even noticed me.

I pushed myself up after Burt had left and gathered Pixie closer.

"Scratch number three," I whispered to her and started up the stairs grinnin'.

Chapter 19

The Announcement

It was a little tougher gettin' up for church the next mornin' but Grandpa saw to it that everybody did. I crawled out sleepy-eyed when I was called, dreading going out to do my chores. I was surprised to see everyone already seated at the table.

"Yer Uncle Charlie took pity on ya this mornin'," Grandpa said.

Uncle Charlie grinned. "Oh, sure. I git the blame for everything 'round here. It was yer Grandpa who slopped the hogs."

"Thanks," I said to both of them.

"Was it a good party?" asked Gramps, addressin' himself to everyone, but to Auntie Lou in particular.

"Real good," she agreed.

"Everybody stay late?"

"Pretty late."

Grandpa decided that it was his turn.

"Thet there young Thomas," he said, "he sure seems like a fine young fella. I was impressed with the way thet he pitched right in and helped ya like."

Auntie Lou's expression did not change.

"You asked him to, Pa, iffen you remember."

"Well, yeah—" Grandpa hedged, "but he never tried to git out of it. Some fellas woulda begged of, hunted up excuses—"

"To get out of spending some time with the prettiest girl at the show?" asked Gramps, his eyes narrow.

"Well, I do admit," grinned Grandpa, "thet it don't take too much talkin' to git a young fella interested in givin' Lou a hand."

Things were quiet for a moment, then Grandpa tried again.

"Still in all, he does seem like a sensible, steady young fellow. They say he's a real good worker, got his own piece of land. Some young girl will be right lucky to—"

"Pa," she said and her voice was gentle yet angry. "That all may be true, but *I* won't be the girl. I *have* not, and I *do* not, and I *will never* in the future care for Burt Thomas. He is vain, borin' and—and a flirt."

Auntie Lou stood up slowly, untied her apron and draped it over her chair.

"I'm goin' to dress for church."

Gramps looked at me and his eyes were twinklin'. Somehow he seemed to know that Auntie Lou was quite capable of handlin' herself.

Nothin' of much importance happened at church. I knew that I had to go; it was one of Grandpa's unwritten laws for our household, but there wasn't much that he could do to make sure that I was really listenin'.

I turned everything off after the openin' hymn. If God wasn't on *my* side, I reasoned that He could jest stumble along without me on His.

I did pull my attention back for a few minutes when there was a stir and Mr. T. Smith stepped to the front. Everyone knew that Mr. T. Smith was the chairman of the church board. He cleared his throat and tried to look like he didn't consider the position as elevated *too* much above the rest.

"You all know," he said, "thet our good pastor and his wife have expressed a desire to retire. We will miss them deeply, but we know thet they have earned the right to some pleasant and—and. . ." He stammered around a bit. It was then that I realized that he had memorized his speech and it had slipped from him. His face started to get red. He finally gave up on the prepared speech and hurried on.

"As I was sayin', we'll miss them, but we're happy about it—for the *Whites*—we're happy that they can retire and rest after their many years of faithful service."

That last part sounded good and I figured that he may have got hold of a piece of his prepared speech again.

"Although we will miss the Whites, we are happy to announce that yer church board has been successful in findin' a replacement. The Reverend Nathaniel Crawford will come to take Reverend White's place sometime in the very near future. We trust that you will all make him welcome and give him yer support."

A general stir followed the announcement. *Nathaniel Crawford*, I thought. What a name! I had a Bible name, too, and so did my Grandpa, but it sure wasn't a mouthful like Nathaniel. I dismissed the new preacher as not worth thinkin' on and went back to my day-dreamin'. It all had very little to do with me.

Reverend White started his message. I listened for jest a minute or two to find out what I'd be missin'. It was on repentin' again. I'd heard that before. This time he was usin' poor ol' Paul as his example of a wicked man turned good. I tuned out. Ol' Paul probably never, ever had anything bothersome happen to him. Why shouldn't he be good?

After church Avery Garrett and I chased a few girls with grasshoppers that hadn't been smart enough to tuck themselves away for the cold weather ahead. Then Grandpa called that we were ready to go home.

I didn't bother takin' off my shoes. It was cool enough now that they felt kinda good on my feet.

I thought of Cullum and wondered if he'd get all his crop in before winter hit. I sure hoped so. I wished that I was big enough to give him a hand. Maybe someday I'd be able to.

The talk at the table was about the new preacher. Folks

were wonderin' where he was from, and what he'd be like, and what he had for family. The only thing I wondered was if he'd still preach on "gettin' ready" and repentance and all. I didn't care much for those kinds of sermons. Something about them made me feel a queer twistin' deep on the inside of me.

I shrugged my shoulders. I really wasn't plannin' on listenin' much anyway, so I guessed it really didn't matter what he preached about. I asked to be excused and went to find Pixie.

Chapter 20

Something Unexpected

The men had gone to town that Saturday, and Auntie Lou and I were enjoyin' a rather leisurely day at home. I was glad to have a full day with Pixie. As little as she was she had already learned to bark on command. I still hadn't been able to teach her to be quiet though.

I worked with Pixie all that mornin', tryin' to get her to roll over when she was told. Her pudgy little legs and round body couldn't manage the trick too well. Lou joined me on the kitchen floor as I worked and played with my dog. We couldn't help but laugh at Pixie's silly antics as she tried hard to twist herself over.

It wasn't until about three o'clock that I decided to chop and haul wood. I put Pixie in her box; I didn't want to take any chances on her getting in the way of the axe or flying wood chips. She needed a nap anyway.

I was busy choppin' wood, admirin' myself for my strength, when I heard a funny sound comin' from the direction of the barn. I had never heard a sound like it before, so I sank the axe head into the choppin' block and went to investigate. I found it all right. An old sow had found a pail somewhere and she had her head caught in it. She was gruntin' and squealin' and runnin' into feed troughs and fences, shakin' her tin head back and forth as she went.

I couldn't help but laugh at her; she looked and sounded so funny.

After I had seen enough of the entertainment she provided, I decided that I'd better do something about it. I climbed into the pen.

I managed to herd her into a corner and get my hands on the pail. I pulled hard but nothin' gave. After several more attempts to release her, I finally realized that I wasn't accomplishing a thing except to work up a sweat. I decided to go for Auntie Lou. Maybe she'd know what to do.

She laughed, too, when she saw the sow, but she got down to business much quicker than I had.

"We've got to pull it off."

"But how?"

"I don't know, but I'll help you. Come on."

She led the way back to the house, and when we got there she turned to me.

"Josh, bring me one of your shirts and a pair of Uncle Charlie's overalls."

I couldn't see what that had to do with gettin' the pail off that pig, but I went to do it. She took the clothes from me and hurried off to her room.

She looked pretty funny when she came down. She had plaited her loose curls into two long braids that hung down her shoulders; that was the first thing that I noticed. The rest of her I could hardly recognize. She was into the clothes that she had asked me to get. The shirt was a mite too small and the overalls way too big, and she made quite a sight. She grabbed a piece of twine from a kitchen drawer and wrapped a loop around her middle. The big baggy overalls were brought in to fit her tiny waist. They bunched up on either side of the string, givin' her a crazy clown appearance. She rolled up the cuffs. It looked like she should have rolled up the crotch, too, but there wasn't much that she could do about that. Pushin' her feet into her gardenin' boots, she took a silly curtsy and said, "Straight from Noo York."

I laughed then. I wanted to before but I didn't know if I dared. She laughed with me, slappin' her funny bulgin'-overall tummy.

"What'd you do that for?" I asked when I could talk again.

She was sober now.

"We gotta get the pail off that pig, and I've a notion that we'll have to throw her to do it. I'm not about to go wrestlin' a pig in a dress."

I could follow her reasoning but she sure did look funny. I had never seen Auntie Lou in anything so ridiculous before.

We had us a real time with that old sow. She was as dumb as she was stubborn. I couldn't figure out why she wouldn't co-operate—at least a little bit. We chased and caught her and struggled—jest to lose her again. Around and around we went. I could understand now why Auntie Lou braided her hair back. Even my short hair got full of dirt.

"We've got to throw her somehow," panted Auntie Lou.

I went for some ropes.

"Now if we can jest get these on her somehow and get her down, one of us can hold her while the other works the pail."

Away we went again. I got one rope on a front foot. It trailed around behind her as I ran after her, grabbin' and strugglin' to get another rope on her hind foot. Auntie Lou tried to help. After a lot of effort I finally got the second rope on. Lou sorta held the pig at bay while I got an end of each of the ropes. I pulled the tension up until I figured that it was jest right, and then I gave a sudden heave against those ropes with every ounce of energy that I had left. It pulled her feet right out from under her and she went down. Auntie Lou and I both pounced at once, pinnin' her to the ground.

"You get the pail," I said between clenched teeth.

She lifted herself back from the pig and grabbed the pail, eyein' the situation to determine jest how the head was stuck and which direction to pull.

"Hurry," I told her, feelin' the pig gatherin' herself together to make an effort to get free.

Auntie Lou grabbed the pail and laid back, pullin' with everything that she had. The pig squealed like we were cuttin' her throat—about that time it didn't seem like such a bad idea.

The pail all of a sudden made a funny suckin' sound, and Auntie Lou went flyin' backwards. The pig gave a big heave and left me layin' on the ground as she squealed her way around the pen draggin' the ropes behind her.

I heard a funny noise from Auntie Lou and looked up to see her sittin' in the pig trough. Potato peelin's and apple cores were splashed up her arms. She even had some of the slop on her face; she sat there blinkin' those big eyes and makin' horrible faces. One braid had broken loose and scattered hair about her face in a disorganized fashion. Uncle Charlie's overalls were an awful mess. Boy, did I want to laugh, but I didn't.

I got myself up off the ground, gave myself a quick dustin' and went over to help Auntie Lou out of her trough-straddlin' position. While I was hoistin' her up, I heard Grandpa's voice.

"Trouble?"

We didn't bother lookin' up, but kept busy dustin' ourselves off.

"That sow had her head caught."

"So I saw."

"You saw it?" I felt like sayin', *If you saw it, where were you?* but I held my tongue.

Auntie Lou stood there shakin' the messy stuff from her hands and arms. Her baggy, borrowed pants dripped peelings and slop. Grandpa cleared his throat.

"It 'pears that we came at a bad time. I brung the new parson here, out for supper."

Both Auntie Lou and I jerked as though we had been prodded; sure enough, there he stood.

He was dark. His hair looked like it would curl if he were to let the cut go for an extra week. His eyes were a dark brown, surrounded by thick lashes and heavy eyebrows. He was taller than Grandpa, but he was slimmer—except for his shoulders. They were broad. The thing that struck me was his age. He didn't look to be more than twenty-five. For some reason I had jest thought that all preachers were old.

Lou was sizin' him up, too. I wondered jest how *her* eyes saw him. No one spoke for a minute and then Lou said, very softly,

"Excuse us, Parson. We weren't expectin' company."

Everyone laughed then and the tension was broken somewhat.

"This is Parson Crawford," said Grandpa, feelin' that all things were now restored to order—but he was a man. Auntie Lou didn't quite share his opinion. Her cheeks flushed a deep rose beneath her pig-slop freckles.

"How do you do, Reverend Crawford."

"How do you do, Miss Jones."

"He's come to supper," Grandpa reminded Lou.

Auntie Lou gathered together all of the dignity that she could muster. She looked straight at Grandpa's eyes. I had never seen her put her foot down so definitely and completely before and I don't think that Grandpa had either. Still she spoke in an even, sweet voice. She even managed a charmin' smile, but everyone knew that she meant *exactly* what she said.

"Supper will be ready in two hours. I would suggest that you use the time to show the Reverend the farm or to have a nice get-acquainted chat on the porch."

Loud and clear she was sayin', "Don't anyone *dare* to step into my kitchen or come near me 'til the appointed time." Grandpa got the message. He cleared his throat again.

"Come, Josh," said Auntie Lou.

On the way to the house she spoke again and her voice had a tremble.

"Josh, I want you to put the tub in my room and carry me up some bath water."

I nodded. I wondered how she planned to get out of those drippin', messy pants without draggin' them through her kitchen. I underestimated Auntie Lou. She gave me another order.

"Josh, when you go in, hand me that blanket from the kitchen couch—out the east window."

She kept right on walkin' around the house. I gathered up the blanket, hoisted up the window, and handed the blanket to her. She threw it around her shoulders and somehow under its cover, she freed herself of Uncle Charlie's awful overalls. Still clutchin' the blanket around her she climbed through the open window, shut it behind herself, and headed for her room. Uncle Charlie's pants lay where they had fallen, drawin' the flies.

I didn't hang around after I had seen to the bath water. I needed some scrubbin' up and a change of clothes myself, so I cared for that and then went back to my job of cuttin' wood.

I don't know jest where the four menfolk passed the time, but promptly when the two hours were up, they were marchin' toward the kitchen. It was cool outside in the fall evenings, and they really weren't dressed for it; I suppose that they were all right glad to get into the warmth of the kitchen.

Supper smelled good, too, and as it was later than usual, everyone was powerful hungry.

Lou hadn't really fussed about the meal. It was the usual, simple yet tasty fare that we normally enjoyed. The table was laid with the everyday dishes. It was clear to me that Auntie Lou wasn't out to impress the new preacher.

She was dressed neatly and carefully in a blue and white housedress, a clean apron tied around her waist. Her hair hung down around her shoulders. It still wasn't fully dried from its recent washin'. Her face was flushed a light pink, but whether it was from workin' over the hot stove or her memory of recent events, I wasn't sure.

She acted the perfect hostess—quiet and polite, lookin' after the needs of those at her table, but no more. The parson seemed to enjoy the cookin'—especially the hot biscuits. He ate them until he seemed embarrassed, and then ate another one anyway.

Like Auntie Lou, I didn't have too much to say during the meal. I was busy lookin' over this new preacher, tryin' to fig- ure him out. I jest couldn't put my finger on any good reason why a young, manly fella like him would want to be a parson. There were so many other things that he could have chosen— like bein' a cowboy or a sheriff or a wrestler. (Avery Garrett had told me about wrestlers. His uncle had watched a match once.) But here he was, a preacher. I jest couldn't figure it out. It was clear that he wasn't in it for the money. Even I noticed that though his suit was neat, it was well worn and even looked to be carefully repaired in a spot or two. No, I couldn't figure it out. I finally concluded that he must be a fair amount crazy—or at least a little slow. As I listened to the conversation, that theory didn't add up either. He seemed bright enough, and pleasant, too. It was all a puzzle to me. I felt real curiosity about the man. He was certainly a strange one.

Before he left he admired Pixie. Now anyone smart enough to see what a sharp little dog Pixie was sort of had one foot in the door with me.

When he turned to go he spoke softly to Auntie Lou.

"Would you and Josh mind walking me to my horse?"

Auntie Lou looked surprised, but there wasn't really any way that she could graciously refuse; anyway he had included *me*. The rest understood that they hadn't been invited and busied themselves at putterin' with the dishes.

We walked out slowly, no one sayin' anything at first, and I was wonderin' jest what this was all about.

"I just want to thank you again for the tasty supper, Miss Jones. I—uh—" he flushed a bit, then a teasin' smile played about his lips. "I—uh—know what an unpleasant situation it was for you, and I apologize. Next time that I come for a meal, it will only be at the invitation of the *hostess*."

Auntie Lou didn't say anything, but her blue eyes widened. She nodded and then looked down for a minute.

"Again, I say thank you," and he touched his hat briefly.

Auntie Lou looked up then. Their gaze held for a minute and then the new preacher turned to me. He held out his hand like I was a full-grown man or something.

"Take good care of Pixie, Joshua. She looks like a real winner. We'll see you both in the mornin'."

I nodded. I'd be there. Grandpa would see to that. The next mornin' was to be Pastor White's final message and the congregation would be introduced to Reverend Crawford. There'd be a potluck dinner afterward, and then the next Sunday we'd have our new preacher. I might even listen a little—jest the one Sunday—jest to see what kind of preacher a man like him would be.

I watched him mount and start down the lane. When I turned around Auntie Lou was already back to the house.

Chapter 21

Parson Nathaniel Crawford

Another week passed. It was rather strange. Not the week really—but Auntie Lou; and Lou bein' the pivot for my whole world, she made everything else seem strange, too.

Gramps developed a bit of a cold, and Auntie Lou fussed and stewed about that, tryin' every remedy that she knew. Gramps tolerated it all good-naturedly, but I really think that he would have rather jest left that cold on its own. It wasn't that bad a one anyway.

Besides, I don't think that it was Gramps' cold that was really botherin' Auntie Lou. It jest gave her somethin' to do with her fidgeting.

Sunday finally rolled around. The breakfast table that mornin' was full of talk of the new preacher, wonderin' what his "delivery" would be like and if he'd be able to help the young folks and still support the old. Gramps added with a chuckle that he sure didn't expect him to have trouble gettin' the young women out. Auntie Lou, who had been lookin' down at her plate and playin' around with a piece of bacon, looked up after that remark, then quickly dropped her eyes again.

I was afraid that she was comin' down with Gramps' cold—she seemed so off-her-feed for some reason; but no one else seemed to notice anything wrong.

Lou suggested that maybe Gramps should jest stay home and nurse his cold, but Gramps would have none of it. He never missed worshippin' on the Lord's Day, he said. He had so much to be thankful for, he maintained, and he planned on bein' there to tell the Lord so. Auntie Lou seemed to think that Gramps could have had his little talk with the Lord jest as well from his own bedroom, but Gramps gently but stubbornly disagreed.

"*Not* forsaking the assembling of ourselves together," he quoted. "We weren't meant to praise Him solo, but as a great chorus."

Then he laid a hand lovingly on Lou's shinin' hair and his eyes were wet.

"Just like your granny, fussing over those you love. I'm just fine, little Lou, truly I am, but thanks for caring."

He leaned over and kissed Auntie Lou on the cheek. Lou knew that she had lost as far as Gramps goin' to church was concerned; but though she still looked worried, I think she was pleased to know that he realized jest how much she really cared about him. She turned to her dishes then, rushin' with them so that she could be ready for church.

Uncle Charlie grabbed a tea towel to give her a hand and they hurried through the mornin' chore. As always, when they were finished, Auntie Lou reached up on tiptoe and gave Uncle Charlie a light "thank-you" kiss on the cheek—Uncle Charlie's reason for helpin' her so often.

Auntie Lou ran up the stairs to her room as though she was really late—she wasn't. Fact was, she had a bit more time than she usually had on Sunday mornin's.

But she sure took a long time a gettin' ready. By the time she appeared again, we men were all standin' around in the kitchen waitin', ready to go. In fact, Grandpa was gettin' impatient. He kept pullin' out his watch and checkin' the time. He was jest ready to call—I could see it comin'—when Lou came down the stairs. At the sight of her we all sorta drew in our breath. She was wearin' her new cream-colored dress that Grandpa had given her for her birthday. The pink trim on it made her cheeks show a rosy pink. Her hair was brushed until it shone and was pinned up in a special way, with little whisps of curls teasin' around her face. She carried Uncle Charlie's shawl over one arm and the locket that Gramps gave her hung around her neck, layin' softly against the creamy bosom of her dress. I looked and sure enough, in her hand she held my lace handkerchief.

"Like it?" She stopped and turned quickly around for us to see each side of her. Her blue eyes sparkled with teasin' and pleasure.

"For my men," she said. "Nellie has been coaxin' me to wear it, and I thought, why not?"

Guess Gramps said it for all of us tongue-tied men.

"Little Lou, you look like an angel—and I'm proud to be able to escort you to church."

He offered his arm. Auntie Lou accepted it and they walked out together. The rest of us followed.

Boy, I kept thinkin', *if Cullum could see her now—bet even he wouldn't think that goin' to church was such a bad idea.*

I wasn't worried about Jedd Rawleigh or Hiram Woxley or even Burt Thomas anymore. It wasn't that I wanted her goin' off with Cullum either, but I was sure that he would take real pleasure in seein' Auntie Lou like that.

The warm Indian-summer weather was back again. It was nice to leave for church without havin' to bother to bundle up so that you could hardly move.

Grandpa pushed the team a bit. We had started later than usual, and Grandpa wasn't one to favor being late for church. We made it on time. As we walked to the door, I could feel the stir around us. Most of the young fellas were hangin' around outside yet—sorta gettin' all the air that they could before goin' in to sit a spell. At the appearance of Auntie Lou there was a great deal of head-turnin', feet-shufflin', and elbow-pokin'. She greeted them with a shy smile and a cheery good mornin' as she passed—jest as she always did, nothin' more nor less.

We took the usual pew. This morning instead of coaxing to sit with the boys, I joined my family, and planted myself between Gramps and Auntie Lou. I could feel eyes on us, and though I knew it was Auntie Lou they were lookin' at, it still made me squirm. I could hear a few girls' whispers, and I guessed that they were probably discussin' Auntie Lou's dress—girls bein' so taken up with what one another is wearin'.

The new pastor took his place and the attention shifted—especially that of the girls. *Boy oh boy!* I thought, *he looks even taller and younger up there behind the pulpit. Preacher has no business lookin' like that. He's supposed to be sorta world-worn and old lookin'.* I hadn't figured out yet what he was to do with his time while waitin' to get old, if he felt a call to preach.

He smiled at his congregation and his eyes seemed to take us all in. Auntie Lou wasn't returnin' his look. She was fidgetin' with a lace corner on her hanky.

The openin' part of the service went pretty much as usual. The songs were the ones that we were familiar with. Mrs. Cromby tramped away at the pump organ in the same fashion as always, and Mr. Shaw boomed out in a bass voice, not always quite on key. The ushers gathered the Lord's tithes and offerin's, and Deacon Brown led in prayer.

It was finally time for the sermon and even the boys my age were quiet and waitin'. I was right curious as to what kind of talkin' this new preacher would do. I didn't plan on really listenin'—jest sorta checkin' up on what he had to say.

His voice was pleasant enough, and one soon forgot how young he looked. His manner and his delivery sort of caught me up somehow, and I got to feelin' like what he had to say had greater authority than his alone.

When I summed it all up later, I felt rather tricked. Really it was the same thing that I'd been hearin' all my life—only put to us in a different way. "God's Glorious Provision" he called it, and went on to tell of man's need because of him bein' a sinful creature and what God had done to care for that need. Yea (that was *his* word)—yea, completely and forever erased the need, by supplyin' man's salvation, through the redemptive death of our Lord.

As I say, I'd heard it all before, but one thing sorta caught me and had me puzzled. This preacher looked like what he was talkin' about filled him with such happiness that he was about to bust. It seemed that he was pleased to pieces that God had gone out of His way to do all that for man. "Mercy," he called it—mercy and grace—mercy bein' the withholdin' of what you *really* deserved, like a woodshed trip if you'd been bad; and grace—the gettin' of what you really didn't deserve, like the extra dish of ice cream when there were six servin's and five people to share them.

At the end of the sermon we sang, "Amazin' Grace," and a look at the preacher's face told everyone that he truly thought it was amazin'.

Willie Corbin went up and knelt at the front cryin' and the new preacher went to pray with him. Now I knew Willie Corbin, and if ever a fella had need to be a bit concerned about some of his carryin' on, it was Willie. I jest hoped that it wouldn't take *all* the fun out of him.

I followed my family out of the pew when the pastor finally dismissed the people. Boy, was the church gettin' short of air. I couldn't wait to get outside.

Willie Corbin sat there at the front, grinnin' from ear to ear, as his ma and pa hugged him, wipin' away tears with the pastor's handkerchief.

At the door there was quite a commotion. Everyone wanted to shake the pastor's hand and say nice things about his sermon. Girls giggled a bit and flushed. Some hurried by, the others openly flirted—jest a little bit. Mothers were the worst. Anyone with an unmarried daughter seem to loiter and gush until I felt a little sick. I wanted to break rank and get out of there, but I knew that I had to wait in line or Grandpa would have something to say about it on the way home.

Finally we reached the door. Grandpa went first, shook the

pastor's hand firmly and said the usual. Uncle Charlie did likewise. Gramps was next. He, too, shook the reverend's hand firmly but jest said, "God bless, young man. God bless." I kinda thought that the pastor liked that better than all those flowery speeches that he'd heard.

Auntie Lou was jest ahead of me. She stepped forward and accepted the pastor's hand—and then she proceeded to shock me half to death.

"Reverend Crawford," she said softly and controlled. "You said that you'd favor our house with a return visit when the *hostess* asked you. Could you come for dinner next Sunday?"

The pastor's face dropped.

"Mrs. Peterson has asked me for next Sunday. I'm—"

"Then the Sunday after?"

"Mrs. Corbin—"

"And then?"

"The Hallidays."

Both of them looked a bit miserable.

"I see." Auntie Lou looked about to move on, then she collected herself and smiled. "I *did* appreciate your sermon."

"Thank you." He looked directly at Auntie Lou, takin' in her creamy dress, pretty hair-do and blue eyes. It was then that I realized that he still held her hand. I guess that they realized it about then, too, for Lou flushed and quickly withdrew it; the parson sort of cleared his throat, embarrassed-like.

Lou moved to walk on by but he quickly stopped her.

"Wait," he said.

She turned.

"Does it *have* to be on a Sunday. I mean, people eat every day of the week, say Monday? Tuesday? Friday?"

Lou smiled. "Of course." She sounded almost apologetic for bein' so dumb as not to have thought of it herself.

The pastor smiled, too, seeming tremendously relieved about something.

"Friday at six?" offered Lou.

"Friday."

He beamed at her and very briefly touched her hand again.

Auntie Lou returned his smile, then turned to go.

It was my turn now. I was sure that after all that, he wouldn't even notice me, but he did.

"Josh. Good to see you. How's Pixie?"

I muttered something that I hoped was at least sensible, even if not intelligent, and pulled away to follow my family.

Somethin' was brewin'. I could feel it in my bones, but I couldn't put my finger on it yet. Whatever it was, I didn't think I liked it.

Chapter 22

Rumors

Grandpa had to make a trip to town on Monday so he inquired if I'd like to go along. I asked if it would be okay to take Pixie, and Grandpa agreed with a smile. He said that he'd bring the dog and pick me up at school to save ourselves a little time.

As soon as class was dismissed I was off out the door, and sure enough, Grandpa was there waitin'. The kids gathered round for a look at Pixie and I showed her off a bit; then everyone who lived along the direction that we were goin' crawled in the wagon and we set off, scatterin' our passengers at the various farm sites along the way. It was a fun trip and I think that Grandpa enjoyed it almost as much as I.

There really wasn't anything much that I needed to do in town, so I asked Grandpa if I could take a run over to the Sankeys to let Pixie see her mama. He said that it would be fine, but not to be too long, so I set off.

I never did get there though. I had to pass the parsonage where the preacher lived, and it just so happened that as I was headin' by, the preacher pulled up on his horse. He seemed to think that I'd come around just to see him, and he grinned from ear to ear.

"Hi there, Josh—and you, too, Pixie," he added. "Right glad that I didn't miss you. Just let me put Big Jim away and we'll rustle up some milk and cookies."

I swallowed my reply that I was on my way to the San-keys—it wasn't like I had to go or something—and tagged along to the barn.

I felt that I should make some kind of comment, so I looked him over—he was wearin' his preacher clothes. I said, "Been callin'?"

"Been over to see the Corbins—that's where I got the cook-ies."

"Pastor White jest used to call on Tuesdays and Thurs-days—unless," I added quickly, "it was an emergency."

"We'll call this an emergency then. Mrs. Corbin hasn't been feeling too well. She wasn't able to be in church yester-day. But I do want to call on all my parishioners just as soon as I can; I plan to visit as many homes as possible this week and next."

He carefully looked after Big Jim, rubbin' him down and givin' him some hay.

"I'll give him water and his chop in about an hour or so," he said. We headed for the house.

"Do you mind, Josh, if I just grab my wash off the line on my way by?"

"Not at all. I'd help you iffen I didn't need to hang onto Pixie."

He asked for an up-to-date report on Pixie's training as he gathered the clothes, and I told him about all her tricks and the next one that I planned to work on. He was anxious for me to show him just how she was doin', and I guess that I was a bit eager, too.

He opened the door and let me precede him into the house. It wasn't blessed with very much furniture, but everything there was shiny clean. He laid his laundry carefully on the table and went about gettin' the milk and cookies.

I received my glass and reached for a couple of cookies from the plate. He took a drink of milk and went right on workin'. He matched his socks and rolled them up together. I noticed that most of the pairs had been mended—some of them many times. He came to a pair with a small hole in one toe and laid them aside.

"Guess I'd better take care of that one before I wear it again." He laughed. "Holes in socks are sorta like sin, Josh. If you don't tend to them right away when they're small and controllable, they grow with amazing speed."

"You mend your own socks?"

"Sure do—socks, shirts, pants, you name it."

"Don't ya hate it?"

He laughed again.

"Can't say that I rightly enjoy it, but I learned long ago that nothing gets easier or any more fun by putting it off."

"How long ago?"

"Have to think on that. I was twelve when my father died. Pa had been sick a fair while, and by the time he passed away, we had used up all of the living that he had set by. Mama wouldn't have him fretting if she could help it, so she quietly sold anything that she could slip from the house without his noticing. After Pa died, my ma had to take in wash to make enough to get by on. I did the collecting and delivering and even some of the scrubbing, as well as any other small jobs that I could find.

"Mama was a very proud and independent woman. And, my pa's cousin lived nearby—big man, big family, but not much energy. His place was unkempt and rundown, and a bit on the dirty side. Mama vowed that no matter how poor we were, our place would never look like that—not as long as she could still draw a breath. So, we both worked hard.

"It was my dream to be a preacher. I saw so many people who were hurting. God had laid His call on my heart when I was a very young boy—and I discussed it with both of my folks. Before my pa died he called both Mama and me in. 'Son,' he said, 'I know it looks a little dark right now, but if God truly wants you in His work, don't give up—there'll come a way.' I assured him that I wouldn't, and slipped out so that he and Mama could have those last minutes alone. Besides, I wanted to get away where I could cry.

"Everytime Mama could lay aside a few extra dollars from her washing, she would order another book for me to read—'to keep the vision fresh,' she would say.

"She was a great little woman, my mama. I'm proud to be her son. She used to worry that I had to become a man at twelve years of age, but looking back now I believe that it was all in God's plan. I had to grow up—to be able to make tough decisions quickly—to learn the importance of following through on one's responsibilities.

"When I was sixteen Mama died and I sold our little house in town and went away to school. I managed to find work— most of the time, and I finally made it. It took me a little longer than some of my fellow students, but God saw me through—just like Pa had said He would."

He was silent for a while; then he looked at me with a queer kind of smile.

"Did a funny thing when I finished, Josh. I took that diploma that I was given, stating me to be a preacher, and I used the last few dollars that I had, to have a weather-proof frame put on it—and then I went back to my old hometown and mounted it on a stake right there between the grave markers of my ma and pa."

As he looked at me I saw a lone tear in his eye. For some reason I felt that I wanted to cry, too.

"Does that sound crazy, Josh?"

I just shook my head and swallowed hard. "I ain't even ever thought of anything that I could do for my ma and pa."

"Your ma and pa loved the Lord, Josh?"

I nodded.

"Then the greatest thing that you could ever do for them would be to love and serve the Lord, too."

"S'pose," I said rather hesitantly, for a funny, uncomfortable gnawin' was busy workin' on my insides. I felt I had to get out of there, but right at that time the parson finished foldin' the last of the clothes and changed the subject so completely that I was soon at ease again.

"Now then, let's see what Pixie can do."

The next few minutes went very quickly. I put Pixie through her paces, and the parson rewarded her each time that she performed with a nibble of one of his cookies. He gave me a few pointers on how to work on her next trick—dancin' on her hind legs. Then I suddenly noticed the clock. I said that I had to rush or Grandpa would be waitin', scooped up Pixie and yelled back a thank-you. I left on the run.

I reached the wagon, pantin', and was pleased to see that Grandpa wasn't sittin' up top, twistin' the reins and frownin'. I crawled up and flopped down on the bit of hay that lay on the wagon bottom, hopin' to be over my puffin' by the time Grandpa showed up.

I didn't have long to wait. I heard Grandpa's voice comin' toward the wagon. He was talkin' to someone.

It turned out to be Mr. Brown, the deacon from our church. They were talkin' weather and then jest as they neared the wagon, the tone changed.

"I was thinkin' on droppin' over this evenin', Daniel."

"Got something on yer mind?" This was Grandpa.

"Don't rightly know what to think. My wife's brother from Edsell County dropped by t'other day. Seems he knows the Crawford family fairly well."

"Ya mean the parson's?"

"Well—yeah. He don't recall a Nathaniel, but he says there's so many kids that he never could git 'em straight."

"So?" Grandpa waited.

"Seems they's not too highly thought of. Shiftless, lazy, dirty—even rowdy—not much account. He couldn't believe that one of 'em ever decided to be a preacher."

"How long has he knowed 'em?"

"Five years—ever since he moved in."

"Maybe he has the wrong family."

"Only one there. Had been another but he and his wife are both buried there."

"So what ya thinkin'?"

"Seems strange to me. I don't know what to think. Henry suggested that maybe this Nathaniel was a smart rascal that figured as how the ministry was an easy way to make a livin' without workin'."

"Don't know much about the ministry then!"

Mr. Brown chuckled, then sobered and responded, "The ministry is what you make it, Daniel. Iffen you're there to help people, you're more than busy, but iffen ya want to coast, I reckon ya could do jest that."

Grandpa was silent a minute, then responded slowly. "Well, Lukus, I shore do hate to pass judgment on a man without givin' him a chance. There could be some mix-up here."

From my place in the hay I was hard put not to jump up and let him know the truth: that the parson was not from the same shiftless family; that he had worked hard and shouldered responsibility to get where he was. But I knew that to do so would be admittin' eavesdroppin' on an adult conversation right there in front of Deacon Brown, and I wasn't sure how Grandpa would repond to that. I figured there would be plenty of opportunity later to casually mention to Grandpa my unplanned visit with the parson. I could then relate the things that we had talked about. I pulled Pixie close and sorta held my breath as well as my tongue.

Mr. Brown went on. "Must admit it has upset me some."

"Now, now, Lukus. Even if he is one and the same, not all apples in the same barrel need be rotten you know. An' we ain't leavin' any room fer the work of the Lord at all. He's restored a lot of rotten apples. We both know that."

" 'Course," said Mr. Brown, " 'course. Jest thought that we should be aware and sorta keep our eyes and ears open fer signs, that's all."

Mrs. Brown yoohooed from down the street and Mr. Brown excused himself. As he turned to go, Grandpa said softly, "And Lukus, I see no need for this to pass on any further than jest to us two—at least fer the present." I could hear Grandpa gatherin' the reins and preparin' to climb up onto the wagon seat.

I got a sudden inspiration and decided to act asleep. I heard Grandpa exclaim and then chuckle when he spotted Pixie and me. He spread a couple of gunny sacks over us and then clucked to the team and we were on our way.

I peeked a look once or twice. I could see that what Mr.

Brown had said truly bothered Grandpa. Sure he was willin' to give a man a fair chance, but even so, he was human, too, and some seeds of doubt had been sown.

I supposed that I was the only one around, beside the preacher himself, who knew the real truth, but it didn't seem too wise an idea for me to share my knowledge at the moment. I felt all mixed up—wantin' to defend the preacher and yet not knowin' quite how, all at the same time. I'd have to sort it out later.

I snuggled down under my gunny sack blanket and then I really did go to sleep, and slept soundly until we reached home.

Chapter 23

Guest Night

I had thought that Auntie Lou was strange the week before, but she was doubly so that week. One minute she laughed, the next she fell into moody silence, fussin' and frettin' over any little thing. She polished and cleaned, and polished some more. Seemed that all of a sudden the whole place was awful dirty-like.

When Friday finally came she spent the whole day in the kitchen fussin' over fried chicken, hot biscuits, and apple pie. The smells that hung in that kitchen were about enough to drive a growin' boy crazy. I could hardly wait for the supper hour to arrive. I knew better than to hang around underfoot, so I waited on the porch with Pixie until I was called for.

"Josh, come and get ready for supper."

I walked in, ready to do my usual wash-and-slick-down-the-hair job, but Lou stopped me.

"I want you to wash thoroughly, Josh, and then change to your Sunday clothes."

My mouth musta dropped open. Sunday clothes on a Friday night? I had never heard of anything so ridiculous. One look at Auntie Lou and I could see that she really meant it, so I didn't even bother to protest—outwardly. Inside I was fightin' it a bit. Silliest notion I'd ever heard.

The other men came in and somehow Lou got the same order across to them. We all went to comply—like so many dumb sheep.

I came down feelin' rather embarrassed. I'd have died if Avery or Willie had suddenly walked in. Lou rushed past me on the stairs, hurryin' to do some changin' of her own.

I walked around the kitchen sniffin' and jest checkin' to see if there might be a stray bit of something that I could sample. Didn't seem to be.

The table caught my eye. It was covered with a pure white cloth, and the dishes that were placed on it, I'd never seen before. It was a little late for decent flowers, so a bowl of apples sat in the center of the table.

I was reachin' for a polished apple when Gramps came out of his bedroom.

"I wouldn't do that, Josh," he whispered. "It would spoil your Auntie Lou's fine arrangement."

He chuckled jest slightly and gave me a wink, "Took her almost an hour to get that just so."

Seemed really silly to me to polish and fuss like that over something that tasted just as good without all that trouble.

We men gathered one by one. I think that each one of us felt a little foolish; we stood around self-conscious, hardly darin' to breathe lest we commit somethin' unpardonable. We were all relieved to hear Auntie Lou's step on the stairs.

She came down wearin' one of my favorite dresses. It was her special blue one and made her eyes look even bigger and bluer. She had left her hair loose and flowin' around her face and shoulders. A small blue bow secured a handful of it at the back of her head. She looked great. She also looked nervous.

She checked the meal on the stove, she checked the table, she checked us men, then she checked the clock. Five to six—and then we heard a horse clompin' down the lane. Uncle

Charlie got up silently to go meet the caller and care for the horse. Grandpa cleared his throat and rearranged chairs that didn't need rearrangin'. I jest stood there wishin' that I could be cuddlin' Pixie, which I couldn't 'cause I'd get my hands dirty. Gramps spoke softly to the flustered Lou.

"Everything looks lovely, little Lou." I knew that this was to try to reassure her.

I didn't mean to help the situation any. I jest blurted out what I felt. "I'm starvin'."

Somehow those two words seemed to break the spell. Everyone laughed, even Auntie Lou, and though she still hurried around with her last-minute preparations, she seemed more her old self.

Uncle Charlie brought in the preacher who washed his hands after his ride. Uncle Charlie followed suit and then we were finally able to sit down at the table. The preacher was asked to pray; and my mouth wouldn't let me concentrate on what he was sayin'; it was waterin' so.

It didn't seem like the grown-ups were in nearly the hurry to get started that I was. They exchanged comments and fiddled around until I felt like suggestin' that it would be quite fittin' for someone to start the chicken.

There were squares of white cloth beside each plate, and I was hard put to know where to get rid of the thing so that I could properly get at my fork. The others took theirs and laid them on their laps, so I got mine out of the way by doin' that, too.

Finally the food started coming around. It was worth waitin' for, I'll tell you that. Don't suppose anybody enjoyed it anymore than me.

The preacher ate heartily, but I got the funny feelin' that he might not even be aware of what he was eatin'. Every time I looked at him he was stealin' little looks at Auntie Lou. He managed to carry on an intelligent conversation with the menfolk, includin' Lou frequently, but I wondered jest how much of his mind was really on what he was sayin'.

It was a slow, leisurely meal, filled with pleasant talk and laughter. When everyone was so full that there was no possibility of holdin' another bite of pie or sip of coffee, Grandpa told me to get his Bible. The story was halfways interesting this time—about some Gideon who sent a whole army runnin' with their tails between their legs, and he only had 300 men to do it with.

Auntie Lou set right to work on the dishes. Uncle Charlie got up slowly and picked up a towel. That preacher got a look in his eye that seemed to say that he would have gladly taken Uncle Charlie's place if he had thought that it would have been proper. Instead, he accepted Grandpa's challenge to a game of checkers.

The checker game and the dishes were finished about the same time. Auntie Lou removed her apron, gave Uncle Charlie his customary peck on the cheek and they joined us. The evenin' went pleasantly enough.

It was nearin' my bedtime when Auntie Lou put the coffee-pot on again. She had some cookies to go with the coffee.

I watched the clock hands move slowly around. It was my bedtime all right; but when Auntie Lou summoned everyone to the table, I noticed that she had a place set for me with a glass of milk; Grandpa jest moved me on over to the table with a nod of his head.

After we had enjoyed the refreshments and the conversation, the preacher said that he really had to be going. Uncle Charlie offered to get his horse, but he said not to bother—he knew where his Big Jim was. He thanked Grandpa for the fine evenin', spoke to Uncle Charlie, Gramps and I in turn (even tickled Pixie's ear and bid her a good-night), then turned to Auntie Lou.

He took her hand and thanked her for the invitation, said that she was a most gracious hostess and a wonderful cook. Auntie Lou didn't say much—out loud. Somehow I got the impression that the two of them said a lot more to one another than what was spoken. I couldn't see Lou's face, but I did see the preacher's, and his eyes were sayin' far more than his lips.

He released Auntie Lou's hand and left. I waited for her to turn around. It took her a few minutes, but when she did her eyes were still shiny and her cheeks slightly flushed. She had a look on her face that I'd never seen there before as she busied herself clearin' away the lunch dishes.

I saw Grandpa and Uncle Charlie exchange worried frowns.

"Leave my cup, Louie," said Grandpa. He hardly ever called her Louie. "I think I'll have another cup of coffee."

"Mine too," said Uncle Charlie.

"Me, I'm off to bed." Gramps covered a yawn. "All your good cooking makes me as sleepy as a well-fed cat. Great meal, little Lou."

He kissed her on the cheek and moved toward his bedroom.

I stirred. Should have known better, but my arm was gettin' stiff from holding Pixie. As soon as I moved, Grandpa caught it.

"Bedtime, Boy."

I nodded and got up; carryin' Pixie with me I went up to bed.

It wasn't long until I heard Auntie Lou pass my door. She was hummin' softly. Normally I loved to hear her happy, but something about this bothered me. I tried to find a comfortable way to lay, but nothing felt right. Pixie finally gave up on me and crawled away to the foot of the bed where she could rest in peace.

It was then that I heard the voices from the kitchen. Worried voices—I could tell by the sound. I crept out of bed and down the stairs as far as I dared, avoidin' the squeaky third step. I sat down against the wall and listened.

"—see it as well as I do," Grandpa was sayin'.

There was the noise of Uncle Charlie sucking in air before he took a gulp of his scaldin' coffee, then his chair landed on all four legs.

" 'Course I see it."

"I've never seen Lou take to a man like thet afore."

"We knew it was bound to happen."

"Sure we knew it would happen; thet's why we been tryin' so hard to steer her in the right direction."

"Too late for any steerin' from us now."

"Not too late!" Grandpa sounded about ready to pound the table for emphasis. "It *can't* be too late," he went on a bit quieter. "This fella's jest a kid, even if he is a preacher, an' he has nothin'—nothin'. Did ya see his suit?"

"I see'd."

"All pressed an' clean, sure, but so thin ya could walk through it—the best he's got, too."

"Ya don't judge a man by his clothes—even I know thet."

"Thet ain't the point! Point is, he can't *afford* a better suit. My guess is he don't have enough change in his pocket at any one time to make a jingle. And iffen ya start with nothin', you sure ain't gonna add much to it on a preacher's salary. The man doesn't even have him a rig to drive—jest a saddle-horse. You wanna see Lou dressed in worn-out clothes, a hangin' on, a-straddle a horse?"

"Now hold on," said Uncle Charlie, and the chair legs hit the floor again. "How'd my *wants* get into this? You know how I feel 'bout Lou. You know what I'd like to see her have. I jest don't see how you can put a stop to this here thing that's a-brewin', that's all."

"I'll have a talk with her."

"A talk?"

"Yeah, I'll have a talk."

Uncle Charlie drew in air again and swallowed some coffee. The chair protested as he tilted back on two legs again.

"Jest like that, a talk, and the girl will plumb ferget thet she ever saw the fella."

Grandpa paused. "No," he finally answered, "no, it won't be quite that simple; but Lou's a good, sensible girl. She'll respect my wishes. Iffen I ask her not to—not to—" he cleared his throat—"not to return the compliment of his favor, she'll abide by it."

"Shore she will. It may nigh break her heart, but she will."

Grandpa got up and moved to the coffeepot on the stove. A third cup? He really was upset.

"Aw c'mon, Charlie. Lou isn't thet far gone. Sure she seems to fancy the young preacher; an' truth is he appears a right fine boy, but Lou has never been one to chase after fellas and—"

"That's jest the point!"

"Ya don't believe in this business of love at first sight, do ya?"

" 'Course not. But iffen I don't miss my guess, there's gonna be some more sightin' bein' done; and she's a gonna look again and again, and then. . . Lou's never encouraged anyone before, but thet look in her eyes tonight—iffen thet weren't *encouragement*, then I've never seen it."

There was a pause.

"And ya think she'd hurt?" Grandpa said.

"Sure she'd hurt!"

"Then what do we do?"

The room was silent for an uncomfortable long spell.

"We weigh it. Is the hurt too much to ask her to pay fer her own good?"

Grandpa sloshed some more coffee into both empty cups.

"Maybe not," he mused, "maybe not."

"Lou might reckon thet love was more important than fancy things," cautioned Uncle Charlie.

"It's hard to pay the grocer with love," growled Grandpa.

"Yeah!" Uncle Charlie heaved a sigh. "But the funny thing is, love has a habit of makin' do even when the pickin's are short."

"Well I don't want thet for Lou! 'Makin' do' ain't enough fer a girl like her."

"Yeah!"

"I'll talk to her."

Uncle Charlie's chair came down on all four legs again, and I knew that they considered the matter closed. I hugged close to the wall and headed back for my bed.

I had heard all Grandpa's arguments to Uncle Charlie. Not once had he mentioned the information passed on to him by Deacon Brown. I knew that Grandpa truly did want to be fair to the parson, but I also knew that it was nigh impossible for him to completely forget what he had heard. He loved Lou and he didn't want to take any chances.

I wanted to keep Lou, too. I hoped that Grandpa's talk would work. At the same time, I felt afraid. Somehow it looked like Auntie Lou would be hurt. I didn't want that. More than anything in the world I wanted her happy.

Suddenly I wished that I was on speakin' terms with God so that I could pour the whole, miserable mess out to Him. I almost envied Willie Corbin. I turned my thoughts around with a firm hand. God probably wouldn't care anyway. He had never cared about my problems before. I pulled the sleepin' Pixie into my arms, buried my face against her and cried myself to sleep.

Of course I could, even now, call Grandpa to my room and relate the entire conversation that I had had with the preacher, but if I did that, then maybe he wouldn't bother havin' that talk with Auntie Lou after all. I felt all torn up inside. It didn't seem fair to the preacher for me to remain silent, and yet maybe my silence was all that it would take to keep Auntie Lou. Somewhere down the road, I promised myself, after everything was settled, I'd for sure tell Grandpa jest what I had learned firsthand about the preacher. Surely it wouldn't really hurt him none if I jest kept quiet for a time.

Chapter 24

Prairie Fire

Grandpa must have had his "little talk" with Lou. I don't know what was said. Lou was attempting to be her own sweet self, but I could feel a tension or strain there. Her cheeriness now seemed put on or unnatural, and at times I saw a real wistful look on her face, like she was yearnin' for something that she couldn't have.

The next Sunday at church she smiled as she shook the pastor's hand, but when he attempted to detain her for a minute, she hurried on. He looked puzzled but was hardly in a position to run after her.

We headed into another week. Our weather still did not change.

It had been a strange fall. Everyone would look back on it and remember it for its dryness. All through the late summer and fall, we had noticed the lack of moisture. Even the farmers who were normally noted for their lateness at harvest had plenty of time to get their crops in and get all of their fall work done. Mr. Wilkes' threshin' machine had sat idle for many weeks and there were still no late rainstorms.

Now it was time for snow—in fact, it was past due. The birds had long since migrated, the animals were wearin' their heavier coats. Nights were frosty and cold, coverin' all but the swiftly movin' water with ice. Ponds were great for ice-skatin' and slidin', but already we kids were tired of that sport and were wishin' that the snow would come so that we could sled and snowball instead.

The farmers all talked about the dryness. At first it had been jest to make conversation, then it was downright concern.

The stubble fields were tinder dry, and the heaped-up dead leaves from the trees rattled like old dry bones as the winds shifted their directions. Livestock had to be watered daily, the natural waterin' holes havin' frozen over and the liquid from the snow not bein' there to slacken their thirst. People worried about the wild animals and their need for water.

It was strange—even the feelin' in the air got to be different somehow. And then it happened.

It was still afternoon, crisp but with no wind and not a cloud in the sky. We had jest been dismissed from school when Avery Garrett let out a whoop.

"Look—there in the west—clouds!"

A general holler went up.

"Snow's comin'!"

"We can sleigh ride!"

"An' snowball!"

"Yippee!"

The teacher heard the commotion and appeared behind us.

"Those aren't clouds, boys. That's smoke!"

"Smoke?"

We looked again; it *was* smoke. I could also see that it was somewhere off in the direction of our farm. Without waitin' for another word from anyone, I lit off for home.

As I got nearer I could see that the smoke was not comin' from the farm but beyond it. That relaxed me some but still I ran on. Before I even got halfway across our pasture, I could see things stirrin' in our yard. Teams and riders were millin' around and more were arrivin'. People ran back and forth between the pump and the wagons. Other wagons carryin' anything that would hold water were at the creek bridge down the road.

I thought that I'd never hold out to reach the yard, but I guess I got my second wind.

You could smell the smoke in the air now, and it appeared from the clouds that were billowin' to the sky that the stubble fire was headed directly for our place.

I stumbled into our yard, pantin' for breath, jest in time to hear Grandpa addressin' the gathered neighbor men.

"I thank ya for all comin' and offerin' to help me save the farm, but it jest won't work."

He was interrupted by protests, but he held up his hand for silence.

"Iffen we fight to save my buildin's, it will take *every* man and *every* team to win. While we're battlin' to save what we have here, the flanks of the fire will get away from us, go on to other farms and then the town. We can't 'llow that. You know it and I know it. We've got to let my farm go and concentrate on saving others—particularly the town."

It was grim business, but the men knew that what Grandpa said was true.

"I'll take a man or two," continued Grandpa, "and Charlie and me will load what we can here and try to drive the stock over across the crik before the fire gets here."

I looked around. The house with Auntie Lou's white curtains showin' at the windows, the barn that housed Bossie, the pigs in the pen, my favorite cottonwood tree, the trail to the crik—everything, everything that I knew and loved would soon be gone.

"Ya best be movin' out, men," my Grandpa said. "We don't have much time."

The men, murmurin' and shakin' their heads, turned to their teams.

I felt sick. My knees gave out and I felt myself goin' down. I managed to slide onto a wood block to make it look like I'd sorta sat down intentional like. I put my head in my hands but jerked it up again when I heard someone shout, "Wait!" Guess all heads jerked up at that one word.

It was the preacher. His horse stood there in a lather, heavin' from the run. The preacher was in his preacher-visitin' clothes so everyone knew that he had been makin' a call on someone when he spotted the fire.

"Aren't you going to try to save the farm?"

"Nope," one of the men answered flatly. "Daniel says we need to save the town instead."

"I think there's a way to save both."

The men looked at the preacher kind of dumb-like.

"Mr. Jones is right, but maybe there's a way that we can save the farm, too. We'll move toward the fire about three-quarters of a mile, where the creek cuts in the closest to the road. Since most of the fire is between the creek and the road, the flames will cover a narrower area.

"When we get there you men with the plows will make a vee between the creek and roads, pointing east, and the fire will feed itself into the vee. That way the strength of the fire will decrease as it moves east, and it won't take as many men to hold each line.

"Mr. T. Smith, you take three men and watch for fires on the south side of the road. Mr. Corbin, you take two men and follow the creek to catch any small fires from jumpers. Those on plows make that vee as fast as your teams can move. All the rest of us will be on hand with water barrels and wet gunny sacks. We'll work both sides of the vee and lick that thing before it gets this far."

In the same hurried voice the parson raised his hand and said, "Let us pray." All the men bowed their heads nervously.

"Dear Lord, you know our need and how much we depend upon your help. We're not going to give you orders about what to do God. We are just going to thank you for being there when we need you. In the name of Jesus, your Son. Amen."

The men had looked doubtful when the preacher had first started talkin', but by the time he had finished his prayer, their faces showed new assurance and they were ready to go.

Teams began to leave our yard—some of them on a reckless run. Uncle Charlie jest barely made it to the gate ahead of them and threw it wide open to give them free access through our field. There was a fence between our field and the Turley pasture, but I knew that the first man there would simply snip the wires so that the plows could pass through.

Our yard was soon boilin' with activity. Men ran for more barrels, pails, water, gunny sacks, shovels, hoes—anything that would aid in fightin' the fire.

Grandpa's partin' shout had been, "Keep an eye on thet fire, Josh, an' iffen it gets by us, you all git." Uncle Charlie had left our team hitched to the rig and tied to the rail fence for jest that purpose.

The dust finally cleared and Auntie Lou and I were standin' alone, shakin'. She was holdin' Pixie as though that little dog were her last connection with a sane world. Gramps came to stand with us.

Gramps had wanted to go, too, to do what he could as a fire fighter, but Grandpa had put his foot down.

"I jest don't want to chance it, Pa." Grandpa had said. "'Sides, yer needed here—in case this don't work."

I took the tremblin' Pixie from Auntie Lou's arms. She stood there silent and white. Her eyes watched the departin' men and horses—one wagon in particular—where the preacher was hitchin' a ride. I didn't know what to say, so I said nothin'.

Auntie Lou suddenly came alive. I wondered for a minute what she was up to and then I realized where she was headin'. The preacher's horse stood where he had wandered after bein' left on his own. He sides still heaved with each breath he drew, and he was flecked with foam from runnin'. Auntie Lou walked up to him. He trembled and moved away a step, but she spoke softly and he let her gather the reins in her hand. Still speakin' she slipped his saddle and hung it on the rail fence; then she proceeded to rub him down with handfuls of dry grass.

The horse responded to her voice and hands, and gradually stopped shakin'. The rubbin' seemed to settled him down, and by the time he was dry his sides had stopped their jerky heaves. Lou continued rubbin' and soothin', talkin' all the while. I don't know what she was tellin' that horse, but it seemed to have a quietin' effect. By the time she had finished and had tethered him, he was ready to eat a bit.

I hadn't stirred. I felt nailed to the spot, unable to think or move. As Auntie Lou walked back toward the house, I looked again to the west. The fire had definitely drawn closer. I wondered if they'd be able to hold it, if the preacher's vee would really work. I shuddered and held Pixie so tight that she squirmed and whined.

"You'd best get on with the chores, Josh."

It was Auntie Lou speakin'. She spoke jest as though nothing out of the ordinary was happenin'.

"Do you want some milk and cookies first?"

I shook my head no, and went in to change my school clothes. Gramps and Lou followed me in. Her face was still pale, but other than that she looked composed enough.

"It could be a long fight," she said. "I'd best get on a big pot of coffee and make up sandwiches for when it's over."

Gramps spoke then for the first time.

"I was wondering, my dear, if we should pack some blankets and clothing into that wagon just in case we need to leave in a hurry—in case it doesn't work."

"It'll work."

Auntie Lou seemed so confident of the fact that I could almost believe it too.

Gramps smiled and let it go, and when Auntie Lou washed her hands and moved to her cupboards to set to work, he did likewise.

I made sure that Pixie was in a safe spot where I could find her quickly if I needed to, and set out to care for the chores.

The smoke hung heavy in the air now and at times you even could see the flicker of the flames.

I did all of the chores. Even milked Bossie. She fidgeted some, a rarity in Bossie. She usually stood still as stone for milkin'.

Instead of puttin' her back to pasture, I jest left her in the barnyard; then I went to the house with the milk.

I knew by the look to the west that the fire had reached the vee. They'd be fightin' there to hold it—all those neighborfolk and Grandpa and Uncle Charlie—and the preacher.

I had counted fifteen of them in all. Not many men to fight a runaway stubble fire, what with the fields as dry as match-sticks, but at least there was little wind blowin' to fight against them. That would give them a little extra time and make their efforts more effective.

I hurried the milk to the house. The pail wasn't as full as usual. I didn't know for sure if that was Bossie's fault or mine.

Auntie Lou and Gramps had finished fixin' and packin' sandwiches. The big black kettle filled with coffee was steam-in' and fillin' the kitchen with its pleasant aroma.

"Josh," Auntie Lou said as I stepped through the door, "set the milk down and bring all of the milk cans. Fill two of them with water from the pump and bring the other one to me."

I ran.

It was a big job pumpin' those cans of water. Guess it wouldn't have been so bad if I wouldn't have been in such a hurry. I was out of breath by the time I got the job done. I couldn't carry the full cans on my own, so I put the lids on and let them sit.

Auntie Lou came out, followed by Gramps. They both were carryin' the baskets that had been packed with sandwiches and cups. I watched as they deposited them in the light wagon that had been left for our escape. They both studied the sky to the west. It was gettin' quite dark by now so the red glow showed up even brighter. The cloudy billows did seem to come from a narrower strip and we began to have real hopes that the men were holdin' the fire.

The remainin' milk can was filled with the steamin' coffee, and it was placed in the wagon with a heavy woolen quilt tucked securely around it. We loaded the cans of cold water, and after Auntie Lou did a final check to be sure that we had everything, we started off.

"We'll go around by the road," Auntie Lou advised and I

knew that she was right. If we followed the road there was no danger of bein' trapped by a fresh outbreak of flames.

I tucked Pixie in a box with Uncle Charlie's old jacket inside. There was no way that I was chancin' leavin' her at home alone.

I drove, Gramps not havin' much experience with team drivin', and Lou wantin' to let me feel like a man.

It seemed to take forever to get to the fire. Now and then the smoke would almost make us choke, and we had to breathe through a sleeve or some other piece of our clothin'. The horses were skitterish, not likin' the smoke one little bit, and it took all of my attention jest to keep them under control.

It appeared that the sky was cloudin' up some, but it was awful hard to tell what was true cloud and what was smoke cover.

We pulled the team up short of the actual fire site, and Gramps walked on ahead to see how things were farin' and to pass on the word that we were there.

He came back almost on the run. They were doin' it—they were holdin' the fire! Little fires were still breakin' out all along the plowed vee, the men not havin' time to plow as many furrows as they really needed. But they were holdin' it, and already it was startin' to diminish.

The word of our bein' there passed along the ranks quickly; the men came two-by-two to take a sandwich and coffee break. Most of the men were more anxious for some cold water. I guess Auntie Lou had figured that when she set me to gettin' the two cans filled.

Two-by-two they came, hurriedly, anxious to get back to their spot in the line, their faces soot-streaked, their clothes smoke-smellin'. Some had small burns and Auntie Lou set Gramps to cleanin' them up and wrappin' the ones that needed it with strips of clean white cloth and strong smellin' ointment.

Auntie Lou poured coffee and served sandwiches and asked the news of the fire from each new pair that came. We found that the fire had given them all a real scare at one point. It had jumped the crik at a narrow spot, and the men fightin' there had had to call on others to help them get the new blaze under control. The men along the road and the vee had had to cover more area then, and it looked for a while that the fire was goin' to win. A few more men had arrived from the surroundin' farms, and that had added, jest in time, fresh strength to the firefighters. They were able to hold it and eventually beat it back.

I saw Cullum comin' for refreshments along with Joey Smith. He looked as sooty as the rest of them, even though he had been one of the late arrivers, havin' farther to come than others. He drank his coffee a little slower than some, and all the time he kept stealin' glances at Auntie Lou. She didn't seem to notice. I asked Cullum how things were goin'.

"I think we've got it," he replied. "Thet was a first-rate idea, whoever thought of it. Thanks to thet, you folk still have yer home and yer farm."

He looked at Auntie Lou again, and I knew that he was truly glad that we still had our home.

"The Turleys weren't so lucky," he went on. "They managed to save their house by concentratin' all their efforts on it, but they lost everything else—all their other buildings, their farm implements, and even most of their livestock."

I felt mighty bad about the Turleys. At the same time I couldn't help but feel relief that it looked like our place would be safe.

Cullum turned to follow Joey Smith back to the fire.

I watched Auntie Lou as she looked anxiously through the smoke at each new set of faces. I could see that she was worried. I wished that Grandpa and Uncle Charlie would hurry and come so that her mind could be put at ease. They came at last, soiled, sweaty and tired, but overjoyed almost to the point of bein' silly. Auntie Lou was right pleased to see them and gave Grandpa a quick hug, but the worried look still didn't leave her eyes.

"It worked!" beamed Grandpa. "We're holdin' it. Still work to do stampin' and beatin' out trouble spots, but we'll hold it. It worked!"

Auntie Lou jest smiled a sweet smile, like she'd known all along that it would.

Uncle Charlie accepted his coffee, but instead of gulpin' it down, he sipped it slowly. I was glad that there was no one else watchin'. It would have spoiled his reputation.

"Got enough fire on the outside without havin' it on the inside, too," he explained.

They hurried back to take up their pails and shovels. Still Auntie Lou kept watchin' through the now lessenin' smoke.

Two fellas came carryin' Eb Crawford. He had had the misfortune of havin' a pant leg catch fire as he tramped out flames. He had rolled on the ground as quick as he could, but he still had a very painful leg. They wrapped Auntie Lou's quilt around his body and Joey Smith was sent to drive him home.

It seemed to me that all of the men must have eaten. Some had even returned for another cup of coffee or a sandwich. The fire was as good as out now. It was decided that many of the men would be free to go home. Only a few would be needed to stay to watch for any unexpected breakouts.

The smoke was still hangin' in the air but not with the same density that it formerly had.

Auntie Lou still paced agitated-like, and I was about to question her when I saw her face light up. It went from relief, to fear, to relief again; and I saw the preacher walkin' through the smoke.

Perspiration had made ugly tracks through the coatin' of soot on his face. His parson's suit was dirty and smeared from trampin' fire, sloshin' water, and shovellin' dirt. Here and there, all over his clothin', little holes had burned through the material where flyin' sparks had landed.

He walked straight to Auntie Lou who was pourin' coffee with tremblin' hands.

"It worked." His voice held intense relief.

Auntie Lou looked at him and her eyes were filled with gratitude.

"Thank you," she whispered and they looked long at one another. I wondered jest what words they would be usin' if what they were sayin' with their eyes would have been said aloud.

Mr. T. Smith came up then and Auntie Lou turned to

serve him. Some of the men gathered around, laughin' and poundin' the preacher on the back, praisin' his plan and the way it worked. Everyone was talkin' and feelin' good in spite of their tiredness and the blisters on their hands and faces. Grandpa came too. He wanted a chance to thank all of his neighbors before he sent them on home. He couldn't voice what he really felt—there jest weren't words—but he tried and I think that every neighbor there understood what he wasn't able to say.

Most of them moved out, drivin' their hayracks or wagons. Through the closin'-in night they went, enjoyin', at least for a while, its welcome coolness.

"Thank ya, Lou, for thinkin' of the men," Grandpa said then. "Guess you can get on back to the house and rest yerself easy. This here fire's gonna hold now. Charlie and me will wait around jest to be sure that no live sparks are still hangin' around."

"I'll wait with you."

It was the preacher who spoke. Grandpa looked hard at him, like he was seein' the man for the first time.

"Be no need, son." He said it with feelin'. "Things are settled now, thanks to you—and the Lord—and you sure did earn yer rest at the end of this day."

"I'd still like to stay if you don't mind." He turned to me. "Josh, would you mind caring for my horse? I left him in kind of a hurry, and I'd sure like him to have some proper attention."

"Auntie Lou already did," I blurted out. "Rubbed him down and everything—but I'll give him a drink. Should be okay for him to have some water now. I'll put him in the barn and give him a bit of chop, too."

I would have said more, but I got the feelin' thet the preacher wasn't listenin' anyhow. He was busy lookin' at Auntie Lou.

It was cool now and as the preacher picked up his shovel and turned to go with Grandpa and Uncle Charlie, I noticed his thin suit.

"Hey wait," I hollered.

They turned.

"I got Uncle Charlie's old coat here in Pixie's box. You want it?"

Grandpa laughed as I hurried to dig out the old coat, but he did commend me.

"Good thinkin', Boy. It's gonna get a mite cold afore the night's over."

The preacher wasn't proud; he slipped into that old coat with real thankfulness. It was really tight and the arms were too short, but it sure beat nothin'.

Gramps and I helped Auntie Lou gather the milk cans and cups, and the empty sandwich boxes; then we headed for home.

It was quite dark now and the horses, eager to get home, had to slow their pace and pick their way carefully along the road. I didn't need to do much reinin'. When we reached home I cared for the team and the preacher's horse while Gramps and Auntie Lou unloaded the wagon and cleaned up the kitchen.

Now that the excitement and scare was drainin' out of me, I felt dog-tired. I dragged myself to the house. When I entered the kitchen, I checked to be sure that Auntie Lou had remembered to bring in Pixie. She had. Then I checked the clock and noticed with great satisfaction that it was way past my bedtime. I grinned to myself as I scooped up Pixie and started up the stairs. I didn't even bother to wash. Auntie Lou's voice stopped me.

"Thank you, Josh, for thinkin' of that jacket. It was a thoughtful thing to do and I was proud of you." She smiled at me. " 'Night now."

I grinned again and went on up the stairs. This time I was gonna get away with goin' to bed unwashed, but I was too tired to even enjoy it. I could hardly wait to fall into my bed.

Chapter 25

Next Mornin'

I awoke the next day to sounds comin' from the kitchen. It was more than jest the usual sounds of Auntie Lou gettin' breakfast. There was male laughter and talkin', and the clink of cups bein' replaced on the table. I jumped out of bed and reached for my overalls. They stunk! In fact, the smell of smoke seemed to hang all about me. I pulled them on anyway and hurriedly buttoned my shirt.

At the kitchen table sat the four men waitin' for breakfast. Gramps was the only one who looked presentable. The others had washed their faces and hands, but little blisters appeared here and there, and their clothes looked just awful.

They were all in a good mood, though, and I figured that they deserved to be.

"Look outside, Boy," Grandpa said when I came down— and I did.

There was our whole farm, alive and complete—and covered with a clean, white blanket of new-fallen snow.

"Snow!"

"Yessiree—started as rain 'bout four o'clock this mornin' and now yer gettin' yer snow."

I grinned.

"Won't need to worry anymore about that fire now," Grandpa went on.

Auntie Lou was busyin' herself flippin' pancakes and fryin' eggs and bacon. Uncle Charlie crossed leisurely to the stove to give her a hand. She let him.

I took my place at the table and lifted hot pancakes onto my plate. I refrained from reachin' for the butter until after we'd prayed. I could hardly wait to introduce Pixie to the snow. I wondered jest what she would think of it.

I ate all that I could hold and the men were still eatin'. They finally indicated to Auntie Lou that they had had enough.

"I really must be going," said the preacher. "I feel badly in need of a bath and some fresh clothes."

As I looked at him I wondered what he would do for a suit come Sunday.

"I'll get yer horse," said Uncle Charlie. He put on his hat and jacket and headed for the door.

The preacher rose from the table and thanked Auntie Lou for the breakfast. He spoke a few words to Gramps and then turned to Grandpa.

"I'm thankful, Mr. Jones—truly thankful that you didn't lose your home."

Grandpa worked at swallowin'.

"And I," he said, "and I. I'll never be able to thank *you* enough for the plan that ya came up with and the way that you worked to carry it out. Seemed everywhere that I looked, there you was, diggin' and trampin' and pitchin' water and fightin' with a wet sack. I'm truly thankful. Any man that can think and fight like that ain't goin' to be stopped by the hard things in life, I reckon. Yer gonna make a great preacher—and I—ah—I jest want ya to know that yer more than welcome in my home—and at my table—anytime."

The preacher extended his hand, his face lightin' up.

"Thank you, sir. Thank you."

He hesitated a moment and then hurried on, seemin' to

sense that he mustn't miss this chance of a lifetime.

"This may seem like taking advantage of the situation, Mr. Jones, but I—I would like to request your permission to call on your daughter—not as a minister, sir," he added with a smile.

Grandpa smiled, too, and extended his hand.

"And I'd be right proud to have you do that." He stole a glance at Auntie Lou who seemed to be holdin' her breath, her hands clasped tightly in her balled-up apron. "I don't think that Lou will be objectin' to the idea either."

It seemed pretty obvious that Grandpa had made up his mind about the preacher. He'd won Grandpa's heart, and I couldn't see that anyone could convince Grandpa otherwise.

The preacher turned to Auntie Lou then. She finally breathed again and managed a smile in response. Her face was flushed and her eyes looked about to spill over. He crossed to her and took one of her small hands in his.

"Wednesday?"

She nodded. They looked at each other for a moment and then he turned and left. As soon as he was gone, Auntie Lou threw herself into Grandpa's arms.

"Oh, Pa!" she cried and the brimmin' tears spilled down her cheeks.

"There now, Baby. There now." He patted her shoulder. I had never heard him call her Baby before.

"I know what I said about him and how he had nothin' and I wanted *more* for you and—and all that; but he's a man, Honey—a real man. He fought that there fire with all his might; and I reckon iffen he puts his mind to it, he'll be able to care, somehow, for a mere slip of a girl, even iffen she does jest happen to be the greatest little gal in the world."

I picked up Pixie and headed outside, stoppin' only long enough to grab my coat and hat as I left.

Sure, I liked the preacher okay, and Auntie Lou seemed to be right stuck on him, and I sure wouldn't withhold anything from Auntie Lou; but, boy, *was I gonna miss her*. I wondered if there was any way that I could be without her and still survive.

I clutched Pixie tight against my chest. I had wanted to

find out her first impression of the cold, white world, but somehow it didn't seem so important now.

I arrived outside jest in time to see the preacher turn his horse from the lane to the road. He had a cold ride ahead. His thin parson suit was still partially wet and the fallin' snow wasn't gonna help his comfort none. Uncle Charlie's old, too-small coat helped some, but left a lot to be desired. Still, I kinda doubted if he'd even notice.

Chapter 26

The Lord's Day and the Lord's Man

Folks were still buzzin' about the fire as they gathered for the Sunday mornin' service. The new preacher had won his way into many hearts, not jest by the fast-thinkin', but also by his ability to pitch in and fight. I noticed several mothers and daughters eyein' him with added interest.

"Ya haven't got a fat chance," I said to myself, and even felt some pride in the fact that he had chosen Auntie Lou above all the rest. I felt sorrow, too, for I still wanted her to stay with us where I felt she belonged.

I was peekin' around to see where my friends were sittin'—and nearly jumped out of my shoes. Way in the back, lookin' kind of embarrassed, was Cullum! All I could figure out was that he was there as a favor to the preacher, seein' how the man was now a hero in these parts.

The preacher wore a suit. It certainly wasn't brand new, but I guess it was the best he could do. It was properly pressed, and the mended places didn't show too much. After the openin' hymn I guess most folks, like me, kinda forgot all about it.

Jest before the preacher was to bring the message, Deacon Brown asked for a chance to speak.

He expressed how thankful the people of the area and the town were to the reverend for his part in fightin' the fire that could have spelled disaster for so many. Because the parson had suffered the loss of his Sunday suit on behalf of the people, the people had taken up a collection to help him replace his loss. Deacon Brown handed an envelope to the surprised preacher, and the people all clapped as they read his unbelievin' and thankful face.

The deacon then went on to say that a fund had been set up at the General Store for any and all who wished to help the Turleys get a fresh start. If anyone had a piglet or a calf they could spare, that, too, would be appreciated.

The service then went on as usual.

As we went through the Sunday hand-shakin' line, I heard the preacher say softly to Auntie Lou, "Wednesday." She smiled and I thought that she had never looked prettier.

The preacher came Wednesday after supper as planned. He had already taken the train to town to shop for his new clothes. There wasn't a store in our small town that carried what he needed. He really did look quite grand in his new suit, though he wore a shirt, not his white collar, when he came to call on Auntie Lou.

They were still talkin' when I was sent up to bed. They didn't seem to pay too much attention to the rest of us, though Auntie Lou did think to put on the coffee for Grandpa and Uncle Charlie. Gramps had given me a knowin' wink and excused himself earlier than usual.

Uncle Charlie and Grandpa took their coffee and moved to the checkerboard in the far corner of the room.

I went up to bed draggin' my heels. I sure would have liked to hear what was bein' said, but even I knew better than to try to listen. The preacher and Auntie Lou spoke kinda soft anyway, and I didn't suppose that their voices would even carry as far as the stairs.

The next day we had more snow, and Grandpa decided

that it was time to change from the wagon wheels to the sleigh runners. I went off to school wishin' that I could hang around and get in on the changin'.

Friday night the preacher came again. This time Auntie Lou had invited him for supper. It was almost more than I could do to sit at that table watchin' him watchin' Auntie Lou with that self-satisfied look in his eyes. She rested her hand ever so lightly on my shoulder as she placed a refilled plate of biscuits on the table. *It's really true*, I thought to myself. *God's gonna take away Auntie Lou, too.*

I excused myself from the table, sayin' that I didn't feel too well—which I truly didn't—and went up to my room. I laid there for a long time tryin' to sort it all out, wantin' to cry and yet not able to. Auntie Lou came up with a worried look on her face and felt my forehead.

"You're not gonna be sick, are ya, Josh?" she asked me and there was fear showin' in her voice.

"Naw," I said, "I'm fine, jest a little off-feed, that's all. I'll be fine come mornin'."

She still looked unconvinced and leaned over me fixin' my already okay pillow and brushin' back my hair. For a moment I felt a sense of victory that I still had the power to pull her away from the preacher; then the anger filled me again—not at Auntie Lou, not even at the preacher really. I mean, who could blame the guy for fallin' hard for Auntie Lou? Still, the angry feelin' gnawed at me, and I turned away from Auntie Lou.

"I'm fine," I said again, "jest need some sleep, that's all."

She rested her hand on my head again.

"I love ya, Josh," she whispered, and then she was gone.

I cried then; I couldn't help it. The tears jest started to roll down my cheeks and fall onto my pillow. I wished with all of my heart that I had remembered to bring Pixie, and then I felt her lickin' my face. She had come lookin' for me.

I drew her close and cried into her fur. At least I still had Pixie. If God would jest leave her alone—keep His hands off—at least I'd have her to love. I didn't even try to choke back the tears but jest let them run down my cheeks, where periodically Pixie's little pink tongue whisked them away.

Chapter 27

Another Sunday

We headed to church in the sleigh the next Sunday. I loved the crunch of the runners on the new snow.

The sun was shinin', glistenin' off the snow on the roadway and the fields. It was gettin' close to Christmas now and the feelin' was already in the air.

The preacher directed the service in his new set of clothes, sincerely thankin' the people for the opportunity of purchasin' them. He looked jest fine.

Already folks had heard that he was *callin'* on Auntie Lou; some of the girls wore disappointed looks, and their mothers weren't quite so quick to shove them forward at every opportunity.

I didn't listen much to the sermon. It was on the love of God, and I wasn't sure if I could swallow it—not with Auntie Lou sittin' there beside me, her eyes on the preacher's face. Instead, I decided to dream up a new trick to teach Pixie, somethin' really spectacular that no other dog had ever, ever learned to do. Already Pixie could beg, roll over, play dead,

sit, and walk some on her hind legs. She wasn't a puppy anymore, but she was pretty small even though she'd grown a lot.
She was a smart dog, and I guess I would have jest about given
an arm for her.

I had a hard time comin' up with something within a dog's
reach that someone else hadn't already tried. The service
ended without me gettin' the problem worked out.

As soon as I could, without bein' too pushy, I made my way
past the preacher, shakin' his hand briefly. I then joined
Avery and Willie in a corner of the churchyard where they
were messin' around in the snow.

"Bet I could take off ol' Mr. T.'s hat," boasted Willie.

"Thought you been to the altar and prayed for God to forgive and help you," countered Avery. "Yer s'posed to be *good*
now, not mean."

Willie changed his tune.

"Said *bet* I could, not thet I was gonna try."

"Does it really work?" asked Jack Berry who had joined us.

"What?"

"Goin' to the altar. I mean, do ya feel different, or anything?"

"Well, it ain't the goin' to the altar," said Willie. I had the
feelin' that he was repeatin' what the preacher had said. "It's
the prayin' thet makes the difference, and a fella can pray any
place."

"But does it *work?*"

"Yeah," said Willie, and his eyes lit up. "Yeah, it really
did. I mean—I used to be all mean and feelin' mixed up inside, and now—now, thet I told God I was sorry and thet I
wanted to quit bein' thet way, I feel," he shrugged, "kinda
clean and not fightin'-mad anymore."

"Ya mean—kinda—*peace.*"

"Yeah, I guess so," Willie answered. "Jest don't feel all sad
and troubled and scared. Yeah, guess that's peace, huh?"

We all stood around Willie. I suppose every one of us
wished that we could feel the things he described. Mitch Turley came over and we left our discussion and went back to
makin' snowballs.

I was turned facin' the church steps where the preacher stood talkin' to old Mrs. Adams. She was almost deaf and he had to lean over and raise his voice to be heard. He stopped in mid-sentence and his head jerked up; then without even excusin' himself he was off on the run toward a team hitched at the side rail fence. I looked over to see what was makin' him run so. What I saw made the back of my neck feel like a snake was movin' up my spine.

There was Pixie, my little dog! Somehow she had followed us to church, and there she was now, runnin' under the 'Toad' Hopkins' team. Now Toad drove the spookiest horses around and when that small dog started dartin' among their hooves, they near went wild.

I started toward the team, too, but before I could get anywhere near them the preacher was already there. He placed a hand on the nearest horse and spoke soft words in an effort to soothe him, but he didn't wait for the horses to quiet down— not with Pixie under there, threatenin' to be tramped on at any minute. No sirree, that preacher went right under, too.

I stopped in my tracks, too scared to even holler.

The horses pitched and plunged and then out from under them—some way—the preacher rolled, and he held Pixie in his arms.

Everyone else had been too busy talkin' to even notice what had happened, and I guess the preacher was glad that they were. His new suit was snow-covered and had a patch of dirt on one pant leg where a horse's hoof had struck him.

He brushed himself off quickly. I noticed that when he walked toward me he limped, though he was tryin' hard not to.

He felt Pixie to make sure that she had no broken bones. She was tremblin' but she seemed unhurt. He handed her to me and I cuddled her close. I finally found my voice.

"Ya coulda been killed."

He didn't say anything for a minute and then, "She's okay, Josh."

"Are you?"

"Sure—I'm fine—just bumped a little. Don't bother mentioning it, all right?"

I nodded. I swallowed hard and stroked Pixie's brown curly head.

"I didn't know," I said, "that ya liked dogs so much that you'd—you'd risk yer life for 'em."

He looked at me then, and reached out and put a hand on my shoulder.

"Sure—sure, Josh, I like dogs real well. But it wasn't for Pixie that I had to get her out. It was for *you*, Josh."

My eyes must have shown my question, for he steered me away from the crowd and we walked off a few paces together, him still limpin'.

"I know how you love Pixie, Josh, and I know how a fella can feel *cheated* when he loses what he loves. You now, you've already lost your mother and your pa, and then you lost your first dog. Lou told me all about it. Pretty soon—well *pretty soon*—I hope that you'll be called on to share the most important person in your life, Josh. You might feel like you're losing her, too—but you won't be. Lou will always love you—always. She's worried about you, Josh. She's afraid that you might not understand, that you'll be hurt and grow bitter."

He stopped and turned me to face him.

"Lou is afraid that you blamed God for your first dog being killed. She's afraid that she couldn't make you understand that God loves you, that He plans for your good, not your hurt.

"It's true that things happen in life that seem wrong and are painful, but it isn't because God *likes* to see us suffer. He wants to see us *grow*. He wants us to love Him, to trust Him."

I thought back about Willie sayin' that he felt clean and not scared or mad inside anymore; I knew that that's what I wanted, too. I fought with myself for a minute, wonderin' if God could really forgive me for the selfish way that I'd been thinkin' and feelin'. The preacher said that God loved me. If He loved me, then I figured that He'd forgive me, too.

"Can we go somewhere private a minute?" I asked.

"Sure," he said. He placed an arm around my shoulder, and we went through the side door into his study in the little church.

Still clutchin' Pixie close, I poured it all out—how I'd been feelin', how I doubted God, blamed God, even tried to ignore

Him if I could. I told, too, about what Deacon Brown had heard and passed on to my grandpa and how I had withheld the truth in a selfish effort to keep Auntie Lou. I cried as I told the preacher, and I think that he cried some, too. Then we prayed together. Willie Corbin was right. It did work! I felt clean and forgiven—and even better yet, *loved*.

I smiled up at the preacher, and I even thought I loved him, too. I was glad that Auntie Lou had picked him. She sure knew how to pick a man.

"Thanks, Nat," I said. That's what Auntie Lou had been callin' him, and I guessed that I'd better get used to it, too—at least until I could rightfully say *Uncle* Nat.

We hugged each other close; then I picked up Pixie and went to find my family. I had something pretty excitin' to tell them on the way home.

Chapter 28

Postscript

Well, I guess that jest about sums up the tellin' of how
Auntie Lou did her own choosin' and ended up with the best
man in the whole county—and how I did my own choosin' and
made friends with God.

Auntie Lou and Nat didn't rush about gettin' married. Nat
was determined to have somethin' to offer a wife, so it was the
next fall, jest after Auntie Lou's nineteenth birthday, that
they became man and wife.

Gramps worked out a couple of little things for them. First
off, he reminded Grandpa that it was quite the accepted thing
for a girl to have her mother's fine things when she married; so
all of our front parlor furniture and the fancy dishes went with
Auntie Lou to the parsonage.

Gramps went a step further, too. As his weddin' gift to
Auntie Lou and Nat, he gave them a fine one-horse buggy.

Grandpa and Uncle Charlie caught the feelin' of excitement about the comin' event, and both managed to find ways
that they could be involved in helpin' the young couple, too,
without offendin' Nat any.

And Auntie Lou—she was about the prettiest and happiest bride that anyone had ever seen. Nat, standin' there beside her with his grin almost as broad as his wide shoulders, looked real good, too.

And then—bless their hearts—they had a surprise for me!

I was at the end of the schoolin' that could be had in our one-room school, so they convinced Grandpa that since I was an apt student, I should have the advantage of the extra grades that the town school had to offer. So when Auntie Lou and Uncle Nat settled into the parsonage, I moved in with them. I even got to take Pixie with me.

I would spend the week with them and go home every Friday afternoon to spend the weekend with the menfolk at the farm. Gramps and I crowded in a lot of good trips to the crik.

The three men worked out their own system for the batchin' chores, and it seemed to work out quite well. Of course Lou still fretted some about them and visited often to sort of keep things in order. She never let me leave on a Friday without sendin' home some special bakin' with me.

So my weekdays were spent with Auntie Lou and Uncle Nat, sharin' in the life and the love of the parsonage, and my weekends were crowded with activities on the farm with three men who loved me. I got the very best of two different worlds. Now how's that for a happy endin'?

A sequel to Josh's story,
The Winds of Autumn, is available
at your local Christian bookstore.